THE EMPEROR TEA GARDEN

Middle East Literature in Translation
Michael Beard and Adnan Haydar, *Series Editors*

THE EMPEROR TEA GARDEN

NAZLI ERAY

TRANSLATED FROM THE TURKISH BY ROBERT FINN

Syracuse University Press

For a listing of books published and distributed by Syracuse University Press,
visit our website at SyracuseUniversityPress.syr.edu.

ISBN: 978-0-8156-1013-7

Library of Congress Cataloging-in-Publication Data
Eray, Nazli.
[Imparator Çay Bahçesi. English]
The emperor tea garden / Nazli Eray ; translated from the Turkish
by Robert Finn. — First edition.
p. cm. — (Middle East literature in translation)
ISBN 978-0-8156-1013-7 (pbk. : alk. paper)
I. Finn, Robert P. translator.   II. Title.
PL248.E615I3613 2013
894'.3534—dc23   2013002406

Manufactured in the United States of America

For my dear girls Ebru and Banu

The Emperor Tea Garden was outlined in *Bartin;* it was written down in various pastry shops and tea gardens in *Ankara* and in some coffeehouses in *Bodrum.* The novel was completely written and completed in the midst of other people.

The Japanese gambling machines which appear in the novel are meticulously accurate depictions of the originals.

The moment I saw the Emperor Tea Garden at the side of the road, the whole structure shook and everything suddenly fell into place.

Just like a season. . . .

Nazlı Eray

THE EMPEROR TEA GARDEN

I wonder what hour of the night it is, I have no idea. It must be late. It is a moonless, dark night. I'm running gasping along roads whose cobblestone block paving strips the heels of my shoes.

I don't know the time, because I haven't passed any railroad station, I didn't come across any square where there was a clock tower in the middle. I am in narrow streets; around me are old buildings with narrow facades.

I can't quite tell whether I am in Istanbul, Izmir, or Ankara. These streets don't seem unfamiliar to me. At one point I seem to smell the sea. I must be in Istanbul. It's as though I am running from Hüsrev Gerede Avenue down towards Beşiktaş. But, as I said, I'm not sure. This could be Menekşe Street in Ankara, as well. I can't tell, I'm confused. The top button of my blouse has opened, and my thin black coat is billowing behind me like a cape. I suddenly realize that one of my stockings has a run.

As I run, I look at the apartment buildings to my right and left. The curtains are open, there are lights burning inside.

꒷ꙮ

A building on my right side caught my eye. I read its name. It said "Arzum Apartments." It had the grime of years on it, as though it had clothed itself in an unknown past.

1

The Arzum Apartments. . . . I pushed the heavy glass and wrought iron door. It creaked open. I went inside. I pressed the automatic lights. A dim yellow light filled the interior of the Arzum Apartments. The stairs were old, some of the steps were worn. I ran up two stories. I leaned against the wall for a second to catch my breath. The lights went out. I found the button with my hand in the darkness and pushed it. That dreamlike dull light filled the interior of the apartment building again. There didn't seem to be a doorman. I went up another story. The light went out. I knew where the button was now. I pushed it and lit the light. The subconscious light filled the inside of the apartment building again. Now I was looking at the names written next to the doorbells. Nizamettin Gürgen, Mehmet Ulubay. I went up another flight: Mesut Dülger . . . I stopped for a moment and rang the bell.

The television must have been on inside. Standing on the doormat, I pressed the bell again.

The door opened.

A woman I had never seen before was standing across from me. She had on a housedress and on her feet were low-heeled open-toed patent leather slippers that had obviously come from Izmir.

"Excuse me," I said. "At this hour of the night. . . ."

"Come in, come in, come inside," the woman said. She stood aside to let me pass.

"Don't take off your shoes."

"But I ran a lot on dusty roads. My shoes are filthy."

"Wait, let me give you slippers," she said; and held out to me a pair of slippers from beside the door.

I put on the slippers and went inside. I went into a small modest salon furnished with old-fashioned furniture. The man of the house got up from the dining table in the corner.

The woman said, "Our guest is here," indicating me.

I had never seen this man with a thin moustache before. I shook the hand he held out to me.

The woman said, "I'm Samime. This is my husband Mesut Bey."

And I said my name.

"Come this way, you must be tired. Let me take your coat," said Mesut Bey. I sat in the chair in the corner.

"I'm sorry to disturb you at this hour," I said.

"We were waiting for you, don't worry, we began," said Samime Hanım. "You were late. . . ."

I was astonished.

"You were waiting for me?"

"Yes, we've been waiting for you for two hours now," said Mesut Bey. "We figured you couldn't find the house."

"But . . ." I said, "But I just entered this building by chance, and I just pushed the bell the same way. How could you be waiting for me? I was just someone running down dark streets. Suddenly I saw the name of the apartment building. The door was open. I came up and rang the bell. How did you know that I would come?"

Samime Hanım chuckled.

"Nothing is a coincidence. We knew that you would come running through the streets tonight, that you would find this apartment building and that you would come here," she said. "Would you like some coffee? You must be hungry."

"Thanks, I'm not hungry."

"A coffee?"

"Okay, I'll have a coffee."

"Medium okay?"

"Yes."

I became pensive.

"You're thinking about something," said Mesut Bey.

"I was thinking, I wonder. . . . I wonder if you've mixed me up with someone else. Believe me, my coming into this street, seeing the name of this apartment building, ringing your bell. . . . They were all just coincidences."

Samime Hanım brought my coffee in a Chinese porcelain cup.

"There's not enough foam on top," she said.

I took the coffee. My hands were trembling.

"Nothing is coincidence, you know this very well," said Samime Hanım.

"Really. . . ." I murmured.

"So where were you running to like that?" asked Mesut Bey. He sat in the chair across from me.

"I don't know," I said. "Believe me, I don't know. I was just running in the moonless night. Maybe I was looking for something, but I didn't even consider what I might be looking for. Maybe there wasn't time to think of it. . . ."

"You were running to get here," said Samime Hanım. "You found it in the end. You didn't miss the building. You came up to the right floor and you rang the right bell."

I took a sip or two from my coffee, and listened in wonder.

"Well, here . . . this place I've come to, where are we?" I asked.

≫◦

"Is that the way the novel starts?" asked Gül Hanım, who was an elderly lady.

We were sitting across from one another in her sitting room. There were brightly colored African violets on the round table between us. Gül Abla had put on her thin gold-rimmed glasses and was studying the pages in the notebook I held out to her. As she concentrated, her deep brown eyes looked larger than normal behind the lenses. She had carefully pinned up her blonde hair. She looked like a queen from days of old. There were rows of pictures from her youth on the wall. The two pictures of her in her wedding gown were more beautiful than all the others. I couldn't figure out how old she was. She must have been more than seventy-five. Her hands, manicured and still beautiful, moved over the pages I had given her. She took off her glasses and looked at me.

"Let me make you a coffee; let's talk. It's an interesting beginning. You wonder what's going to happen," she said. She struggled up from her place and headed over to the kitchen. She was a woman who had seen better days. Her furs hung on the coat rack in the corridor. Her high patent leather boots were next to one another on the floor. In the parlor, which she kept closed up, was a small pool with a fountain. She rarely opened that room. On the nights that I stopped by, we sat opposite one another in this little room. When she went to the kitchen to make me coffee, I quietly plucked a leaf from the most colorful of the African violets and stuck it in my bag.

This old house sheltered many memories. The pictures on the wall, the divan in the corner covered with a *kilim*, Gül Abla's green worry beads, stuck in a corner of the calendar, my photograph taken under the eucalyptus tree in my garden in Bodrum. Since it was autumn in the picture, I was wearing the Angora jacket I had bought from the lady who sells wool on Tunalı Hilmi in Ankara. . . .

≈o

"You're very distracted tonight," said Samime Hanım. "What are you thinking about?"

"Nothing," I said. "I thought of an old friend of mine for a minute. Her house was very close to mine in Ankara. I used to stop by when I was free on Sundays and sometimes in the evening after the television news. She had beautiful African violets. If I forgot her, she would get annoyed and reproach me."

"What was her profession?" asked Mesut Bey.

"She was a retired teacher. And she worked for many years as a labor attaché abroad. She knew good German. Sometimes we would talk about Berlin together."

"Do you see her often?" asked Samime Hanım.

"Not anymore," I said slowly.

"Why?"

"She died. Suddenly. One night they called me from the police station. She had a little card on a string around her neck with my name and telephone number on it. She had died two days before. The neighbors found her. She had a heart problem. I'd been neglecting her for a while. I can't forgive myself."

"It's death, what could you do about it?" said Samime Hanım.

"I could have paid more attention to her. I could have called her every day. . . . I didn't do anything." My eyes teared over.

≫∘

Gül Abla brought my coffee in an old fashioned tray with flowers on it. I looked at the plant worriedly to see if the place where I had broken off the leaf was obvious.

Gül Abla took her place across the table and stared at me.

"Well, drink your coffee and light up a cigarette. Relax a little."

I took a cigarette out of my pack and lit it up.

"I smoked for years, then I gave it up," said Gül Abla. "I smoked menthol cigarettes."

Several rings twinkled on her fingers. She carefully did her own manicures, she had told me.

"If I turn my cup over, will you read my fortune, Gül Abla?"

"Just smoke up your cigarette, and I'll look at it."

One day she said to me, "You know, I live your life right along with you. I experience all your excitement, feelings, joys, and disappointments in this room. You come before my eyes some nights and I know you're upset. As I hear you tell me what's going on, I live what you're going through."

Just then I thought of some words from Luigi Pirandello: "There is someone who is living my life and I know nothing about that person."

This sentence from the famous Italian playwright is so affecting and so frightening.

I looked closely at Gül Abla sitting across from me. She was flattening the wrinkles on the tablecloth, and looking at me as she continued to talk.

"Yes, I live your life right along with you. Minute by minute, second by second. As I said, when you're happy I feel it, when you're upset I know right away. . . ."

"Gül Abla," I said, "you know me so well, don't you?"

"Don't I?" she said, "I know you as if I had given you birth."

I drank up and finished my coffee.

I had known her for four years. She more or less knew everything about my life.

How did I meet her? In a beauty salon, among all the women waiting there. Years ago . . . she was sitting in a corner. We had spoken. She gave me the address of her house.

One Sunday, on one of those silent, motionless evenings that only happen on Sunday, I went to her home. We talked for a long time and became friends.

She didn't go out much. First she welcomed me in her closed up parlor. It was full of furniture. In the middle was that strange little pool with the fountain. There were knick-knacks and pictures decorating it everywhere, and thick velvet curtains always gave the room a dim feeling.

Later when I went to her, I preferred to sit in that little room where we always sat. There was a comfortable armchair, with the old phone behind me. Occasionally we'd turn on the television and talk about politics. She was someone who had experienced a lot in her life. Thick braids of her blonde hair from the first time she cut it were hanging in a frame on the wall.

If I began to neglect her a little, she would call me up and complain.

Every summer for three weeks she would go to a mineral spa and send me a card from there.

"Gül Abla," I said.

"Yes, my dear."

"I'm going to tell you something important."

"I'm listening."

꙳

Samime Hanım said, "I brought you the coffee first, but you must be hungry. There are cold olive oil dishes ready. Let me put something on a plate. . . ."

"Thanks, I'm not at all hungry," I said.

"Sit back and relax. You seem a little tired."

"I got here by running along roads I don't know. Just look, the heels of my shoes are all shredded. . . ."

"When did you last see Gül Hanım?"

"I called her up a few days before she died to see how she was. Really hot summer days weren't good for her. She kept talking about her heart. Then I got the news that she had died. At midnight. I had just come home. You know, just as I told you, an officer called me from the Kavaklıdere Precinct.

"'What were you to her?'

"'An acquaintance.'

"'Not a relative or anything?'

"'No, just an acquaintance. Do you know why she died?'

"'It was her heart.'

"'The funeral?'

"'She was buried. We couldn't reach you,' said the officer.

"'When?'

"'Yesterday at noon.'

"I hung up the phone."

Samime Hanım asked: "Did you visit her afterwards?"

"Her grave. Yes."

"How did you find it? Did you ask at the precinct house?"

"No," I said. "I already knew where her grave was when she was alive."

Samime Hanım was surprised. "How could that be?" she asked, staring at me in astonishment.

"It's a strange story," I said. I went to the Old Cebeci Cemetery one day. It was springtime. The lilacs had opened in the cemetery, birds were singing in the trees. It's a cemetery where people from a long time ago are at rest, ones who were buried between 1942 and 1944. I was walking along the narrow path lost in thought when a new grave caught my eye. "Zeliha Gül Korcan" was written on it. I was shocked. I ran out of the Cemetery, jumped into a taxi and went to Gül Abla's house.

I rang the outside bell again and again. The automatic door opened with a long slow buzz. I went up the steps two by two. The door was half open, as it always was when she expected me. I tapped with the little brass door knocker. The door opened.

Gül Abla stood before me. She was smiling sweetly at me.

"Come, come in," she said. "Take off your shoes right there. They're full of mud."

"Gül Abla," I shrieked. "I've seen the most awful thing. A little while ago . . . A grave! Your name was written on the gravestone. I felt awful!"

"Are you coming from the cemetery?"

"Yes."

"Did you go to visit your grandmother?"

"Yes. I went to visit her, my uncle, and my grandfather. I wanted to lose myself there in that world on this spring day. To wander amidst the forgotten gravestones, to feel the scent of the lilacs. . . . Then I came across that grave. I was very frightened."

"Don't be afraid," said Gül Abla. She sat in her chair. And I was sitting across from her. My eye caught for a moment on the purple and pink African violet plants.

"What a strange thing," said Gül Abla. "You got to see my grave while I was still alive. If I had told you the way, you would never have found it. In that crazy old graveyard you just came across it. See!"

"Is that your grave?" I asked in astonishment.

"Yes, I arranged for it. I got it ready."

"Oh Gül Abla," I cried. "You should have spent that money on something else."

She had put on her glasses. Her eyes seemed larger now.

"Some things have to be prepared," she said. "I bought it, I arranged it. There's an empty plot next to it. Keep it in mind, in case someone wants to buy it. I'll sell it. Since I have nobody of my own."

"I felt weird, seeing that grave. . . . Well, let's talk about something else," I said.

"Wait, let me make you a coffee."

"Sit," I said. "Sit, Gül Abla. I have to tell you something important."

She laughed.

"I know, tell me," she said. "Tell me."

≫●

I was walking along the narrow paths among the gravestones, some of them crooked, in the Old Cebeci Cemetery. The season was autumn, and the yellow leaves were crunching beneath my feet. I was seeking Gül Abla's grave. I just couldn't find it. I must have gone on the wrong path. On the old gravestones, the porcelain photographs split by the pitiless hands of time were staring at me. Young, beautiful women, with thick eyebrows and wavy black hair, fixed expressions, men with deep looks, their hair combed, their thin moustaches trimmed . . . pictures of the dead people taken at the most beautiful age of youth . . . these porcelain medallions made from photographs taken when they were living, full of hope, waiting for tomorrow in excitement.

The leaves made a soft sound in the wind. I must have gone into a part of the cemetery I'd never seen before. A sparrow was drinking from a gutter filled with water. I read the inscription on a grave I passed by that went something like this:

> My dear son Celal
> You burned with the fire of love
> You fell into despair
> You threw yourself from the window
> Was it worth it, my dear child
> You burned us as well.
>
> Your Father

I turned back and looked at the dates written on the tombstone.

CELAL DÜLGER
1947–1967

He had died at age twenty.

Celal Dülger . . . Celal Dülger . . . I wandered a while more running this name around in my brain. I had come back to the place where Celal's grave was. His passionate eyes were on me.

A feeling I couldn't describe was drawing me like a magnet to this grave. I couldn't pull myself away. I sat gently down at the edge of the grave.

The air had cooled, and an autumn breeze that made me shiver came up. I was trembling a little. The dimness of twilight fell around me.

"You sat on the stone. You'll catch cold," a voice said.

Startled, I sat up and looked around, but there was no one to be seen.

"If you're not careful, you'll get sick. The evenings here are damp and cold," the same voice said.

I stood up. I brushed a bug off my skirt. It knew it must be a guard from the cemetery talking to me, but I couldn't see where he was.

"If you're looking for me, I'm here," he said.

I lifted my eyes in fear and looked at the porcelain photograph on the stone.

His eyes seemed somehow different. They were looking softer now.

I turned my head to where the tree was. I was seeking some shadow, some movement.

"I'm here, I'm talking to you," said the sound.

I saw that the porcelain photograph was slightly smiling at me.

I had a moment of total terror.

It must be a play of the light striking the picture in the gathering darkness.

"Don't be afraid," said the young man in the porcelain photograph. "You're not afraid of me, are you? Nobody's come to visit my grave for many long years. The loneliness of a dead person . . . You can't understand it. Months, seasons, years go by and you're dead now. You just wait, and you don't know what you're waiting for . . . Because there's nothing left to wait for. They took your watch off your arm years ago. Yes, I've been living the loneliness of the dead here for years. They used to say prayers for me. That's over too. I've been forgotten for a long time," he said.

"Celal Bey," I said. My lips were dry. I was dizzy. I had no idea what to say.

"How's it outside? How's life?" asked the porcelain photograph.

"It's completely different outside," I said. I wasn't afraid of him anymore. The porcelain photograph of a lonely young man who had committed suicide for love thirty years ago was talking to me, was asking about the life he had left long ago.

"Life is going on at full speed out here," I said. "Every minute, every second everything can change. That river we call life is bubbling and flowing.

"So, that's the way it is." His voice was sad. "Don't go," he added. "Please don't go. Let's talk. Tell me about life. I left life behind at a very young age. . . ."

"I'm not going, I'm sitting here," I said. "I'll try to tell you about life. But how good can I be? Why did you leave this world? I read what's on the stone. Why did you think of doing such a thing?"

"I was crazy in love with her," he murmured. His voice seemed to have gone back to the past for a minute.

"It was a mad love. It hits people in a different way when they're so young, you know. . . . She was very beautiful. I still remember her. Her laugh, her long, thin fingers . . . Afterwards, she came to my grave once. She was crying. I realized she felt guilty.

"'Celal, why did you do this?' she was sobbing.

"But I had heard that she loved someone else. She didn't even see me anymore. This was such a horrible thing, you know. An officer with an ironed uniform and braid on his collar. She was older than me. She was the most beautiful woman I had ever seen. The scent of jasmine came from her black curly hair to your nose.

"She said to me, 'Celal Bey, I love somebody else. I never loved you . . . leave me alone, don't walk by my house in the evening anymore,' she said. At that moment I was destroyed. I didn't know what to do. She couldn't belong to anyone else. But when she said these words, she was so at ease, so far from me. Then one night. . . ."

"Don't tell me! Don't tell me! I know what you did," I cried out. My heart was full of anguish. He continued to talk.

"I remember the stones of the street quickly coming at me, the world upside down, and the trunk of a tree. Everything happened very quickly. Then I died," he said.

What I had heard had upset me. He had told me of a dead love, passion, despair, and the moment of death.

He hadn't had enough of life, this I understood. He had told me all about his youth, his madness, his love, his life, and his moment of craziness.

"If only you could come out of here and come back to life again," I murmured. "You lived very little. You would have had other women in your life. Maybe women that you would have disappointed. You would have forgotten her."

"I know. I know this now. But at that time, in those moments, how could I have known?" he said.

A branch crackled behind me. I jumped up. Behind me there was a middle aged man standing at the base of a tree.

"This grave has affected you. You've been sitting here for hours. Did you know him?" he asked.

"Have I been sitting here for hours?" I asked in astonishment.

"Yes, you've been here for two hours. I've been watching you. I was behind that tree. Did you know him?"

"No, he was someone I didn't know at all," I said.

"You spoke to him. . . ."

"Yes, I did."

There was a silence.

"Did you know him?" I asked. "But how would you know him, from years ago . . . ?"

"No, I know him," said the man. "We have had many days together."

I was surprised.

"Who are you?"

"My name is Irfan."

"Irfan."

"Yes, Irfan the Paradise guard."

I couldn't believe what I had heard. The young dead person whose tombstone I had randomly read had spoken to me, and told me about his hopeless love. Now this man in front of me was telling me that he was Irfan the Paradise guard.

"What do you do?" I murmured.

"I wait at the gate of Paradise," he said, in a natural way. "I control who goes in and out."

"So you control who goes in and out. . . ."

"Yes, that's my job"

"Okay, are there ever people who leave?" I asked with interest.

"Well, sometimes, with permission," said Irfan.

"Really? I've never heard this."

"Nobody knows this. It's not talked about very much. It would get around then."

I was trying to comprehend.

"Could you do me a favor?" I asked. "Could we get this young dead person out? He's very interested in life. He couldn't live, he didn't have his fill of life. . . . How could we do this, I wonder?"

Irfan stopped for a moment.

"Do you want to put him back in life so much? What is he to you?" he asked.

"I told you, he's nothing to me. But what he told me affected me."

"I really don't show myself to anyone. You know what I mean. . . ." said Irfan.

"I know."

"Maybe I could do you a favor."

"What?" I cried.

"I'll let him go. But with one condition. I'll be with you. I have to be with you wherever you go. Otherwise he'll run away into life and disappear."

A magpie called in the distance.

"News. . . ." said Irfan.

"You stay with us. What's the harm," I said.

"Thank you . . . Okay, then turn a little around. Turn some more. Look somewhere else for a bit. . . ."

"Okay."

I gazed my eyes over the branches of the tree, looking for the magpie that had just called. It had disappeared. I couldn't see it at all. And its call was gone.

"Okay, you can turn," said Irfan.

I turned around.

The young man in the porcelain photograph was standing next to Irfan. The two of them stood side by side, staring at me.

In the twilight falling on the cemetery, they were two very interesting men. . . .

Irfan said, "God willing, this thing won't get out. I hope you keep your mouth shut."

"It won't get out! It won't!" I cried.

"Easy," said Irfan. "They'll hear. . . ."

Celal had on a well-cut silk shirt yellowed by age, and dark grey pants. He was tall. He threw back his black hair with his hands.

"Let me walk a step or two," he said.

He stared around him, at the trees, at the cemetery that was gradually being buried in darkness.

"Every part of me is numb. I haven't walked for thirty years. The air is wonderful. It's evening. In a little bit the stars will come out," he said. It was as though he were under a spell. He took deep breaths.

I looked at him for a while.

He was breathing in the individual songs of the birds in the distance, the sound of the wind, the slow descent of the night, and the crackling of the leaves beneath his feet.

Irfan was leaning against a tree, slipping his worry beads through his fingers.

I was very excited by what I had just experienced.

"Come on!" I yelled. "Come on, let's get out of here!"

Celal said, "Let's wait a bit. My lungs seem like they're parched for air. Let me get used to the world. Let me get used to life again. There are so many sounds around; it's like the plants and the trees are talking, can you hear them?"

But the Old Cebeci cemetery was very quiet. It had become quite dark.

Irfan said, next to me, "His senses are very sharp now. He sees and feels everything differently than we do. He was under the earth for thirty years."

"How strange," I mumbled. "He thinks this is life. But there's no life here. This is a forgotten world. Sad and silent."

"Just ask him," said Irfan. "He's taken a step towards life. Look how's he's looking at the sky, like he's drinking in the black night. . . ." Truly, Celal had raised his head to the heavens and was staring mesmerized at the stars that began to appear one by one as the night fell upon us.

Irfan the Paradise guard was pulling on his rosary, which clicked through his hand.

"Thank God. It's evening again," he said.

Irfan had on a mouse gray outfit with metal buttons in front that looked like a uniform. There were thin black stripes at the cuffs. When he saw I was looking at him, "This is our winter uniform," he said. It's autumn now so last week they gave out the winter uniforms."

"Where do you live, Irfan?"

"In the Paradise guard staff housing."

I had never heard of the Paradise guard staff housing.

"The Paradise guard staff housing? Where is it, I've never seen it," I said.

Irfan said, "Well, it doesn't just appear to everybody. Like it says, Paradise Guard Staff Housing."

"The moon's coming up, little by little! What an incredible thing!" Celal shouted.

The sky was coming alive. The stars were out, the moon was rising among the branches.

"Should we go?" I asked Celal. "Have you gotten used to the world a little?"

"I have, I have," he said. "I'm thinking of a thousand things."

"Like what?"

"I wonder if I can find her. I'd like to see her . . . ," he said.

"Who?"

"Adviye."

"Adviye?"

Slowly, "Her name was Adviye," he said. "Adviye the Beauty . . . The one who left me, who fell in love with an officer . . . You know, I said her hair smelled of jasmine. . . ."

"Where would we find her?" I asked. "Who knows where. . . ."

"Right," said Celal. "It's been a long time. Who knows where she is now. . . . If I could see her once, just once. . . ."

Irfan said, "It would be hard to find her. Forget about her. You'll find somebody else. What good would it do you to see that women who caused you such pain, who more or less took your life from you?"

Celal was pensive.

"I don't know, I don't know. But I want to see her. I waited years for her to come. It was terrible waiting. I knew she wasn't coming, but I still waited.

"Maybe one day she'll come," I said.

"I waited every spring, I waited in the snow, she didn't come," he said.

"Come on, let's get out of here," I said. "It's really become cool. Come on, let's walk down that path. I can't find the exit, I think we've lost the way."

≫ₒ

Gül Abla was carefully cutting a columnist's article from the paper.

"I really like what this man writes. I'm going to save it. I'll bring you a sweet. Squash dessert. You like it. I just put the walnut on it. Wait, I'll just bring it." She said.

"Come, sit, Gül Abla," I said.

"Wait, let me get the sweet, then I'll sit. I made it because you like it. It's like candied chestnuts. Here, your napkin's right here," she said.

She sat across from me, in her usual place.

"Gül Abla," I said.

"What, dear?"

"There are things I have to tell you. Important things are happening. Connected to my life. I have to tell them to you right away. I need your advice. I don't want to lose time. I'm in an awful way, really; every minute, every second that passes is important. I'm in the middle of something where I'm afraid I'm not going to be able to hold on. I don't know what to do. Help me," I said.

"I know. I know you're in the middle of a storm. Tell me . . . You are not telling me anything!"

"I will tell you," I said. "But first of all, I want to ask you something. Did you ever know anyone named Adviye Hanım?"

Gül Abla stared closely at me.

"Adviye Hanım? Where did you get that from? Is what you have to say connected with this Adviye Hanım?"

"No, there's no connection. The things I have to say have to do with me. . . ."

"Why did you think of Adviye Hanım now? I wonder who Adviye Hanım is. I know two Adviye Hanıms, but they're old people. You wouldn't know them. . . . Why did you ask?"

"You know two Adviye Hanıms?"

"Yes," said Gül Abla. "They were both beautiful when they were young. One is Adviye the wife of the judge, the other is Adviye the doctor's wife."

"Which one was a dark beauty?"

Gül Abla: "When they were young they were both beautiful. The judge's wife was famous for her dark curly hair. She had clear, white skin," she said.

"That's her," I said. "That's Adviye!"

"She played the lute beautifully," said Gül Abla. She was lost in thought for a moment. "She had deep eyes . . . Long black lashes."

"Do you still see her?"

"I still see her. She's my old friend."

"Would you take me to her?"

"I will," said Gül Abla. "I'm interested. Why do you want to see Adviye Hanım so much?"

"I'll tell you everything later. When are you going to take me to Adviye Hanım?"

"Wait a minute. I have her number written down over there in my book. Give me that book a minute . . . not that one, the one underneath, with the blue cover. I'll call her."

"Can we go right away?"

"We can't go right away, we'll go tomorrow, if she's available," Gül Abla said.

I was playing with my squash dessert.

"You didn't have any of the dessert. You're just playing with your fork with it. Tell me, what's going on?"

"I'm like a pilot making a blind landing," I said. "The throttle's in my hand, I'm in a panic, I can't find anywhere to land. The gauges aren't working, my radio is out. The fuel is about to give out. I can't get in touch with any tower. I'm lost in the darkness."

I was staring.

She was staring at me.

"Was there something between you?" she asked.

"Yes, I hurt him, I lost it. He was shocked, he didn't know what to think. The telephone calls stopped, the person who always was in touch became quiet. There were no messages on my machine anymore. Time is going by and I'm struggling with this hopeless waiting."

"You just wait," said Gül Abla. "Don't call. You wait."

"But maybe he doesn't know that I'm in such pain. I felt like I have a knife stuck in my brain. I keep losing blood."

"What are you saying?" cried Gül Abla. "When you say things like that to me you have no idea how upset I get. It's like the edge of that sharp knife just went into my brain."

"I know," I murmured. "You're living my life. . . ."

"What did you say?"

"Nothing. I was just thinking. I didn't say anything."

"If he really loves you, he'll call," Gül Abla said. "You wait."

I sighed deeply.

"You're very emotional. He must know you. Time will solve everything," she said.

"Time . . . this is a terrifying thing, Gül Abla. How can I leave everything to time?" I shouted. "I'm afraid. I'm afraid of time. Time makes you forget."

⇒₀

We were walking along the dark path.

Irfan said, "How strange, he hasn't forgotten that woman in all this time." With his head he indicated Celal, who was walking in front of us. "It's been such a long time. Almost half a century. Half a century all by himself, without anything happening. But that woman is still right there in his head."

"It's because he never lived," I said.

"You think so . . ." said Irfan.

We were walking downhill along the path. Irfan suddenly grabbed my arm.

"My God! Look at that place with all the lights over there! What is it? Do you think light from heaven has come down on one of the tombs? Or is it phosphorus coming up from one of the dead? What unusual colors . . . yellow, purple, green. They blink on and off. I've never seen colors or lights like that here. Except for once years ago, in the middle of a hot night, the layer of phosphorus that appeared over the tomb of a soldier. It was like fog. But that's not like what we see here!" he shouted.

I looked where he pointed.

There really was a blinking mass of colors off in the distance.

"Maybe it's a flying saucer?"

"I don't know. . . ."

Celal also saw this tumult of color in the silence and darkness.

"Look!" he said. "There's something going on over there!"

I heard soft music too, as though someone were calling us. The three of us were walking towards this brightness across from us. It was as though we were magnetized.

"It's like an illuminated funeral plot . . . ," said Irfan. "But in all this time I've never seen an illuminated funeral plot."

"Some kinds light up," I said. "With green bulbs. But what we see doesn't look anything like that. It's very lively and colorful. It must have something to do with life, not death."

"The music . . . do you hear the sound of music?" Celal asked.

We were very close to the blinking colored lights now. I couldn't hold myself back and began to run over towards it.

"Stop!" said Irfan the Paradise guard from behind me. "Stop, aren't you afraid? Let's not separate from one another."

"I'm not afraid. Come, come, I know what it is!" I said.

I knew what the mass of lights in front of me, the gleaming toy, was. It was an incredible, wonderful thing!

"What? Tell us, what is it?" Celal asked in excitement.

"It's the latest 1966 model Japanese Sigma electronic slot machine!" I shouted. "They have the same one in the Venus Casino. It's a very unusual machine. It draws people like a magnet. It can take all your money or make you rich in a minute. You can't escape its spell. Like a dangerous woman. Its name is Marine. There are dolphins, swordfish, crabs, red sea stars, and yellow lobsters constantly whirling through in it. Then the bags of gold suddenly come. Two bags of gold, if you're lucky three bags of gold, and sometimes, even four. The bags begin to tremble and turn around. You start to push the buttons in front of you. The bags of gold start to open. Some of them are full and some of them empty. If you find the gold with the mark on it, brand new bags appear. You keep on pushing the buttons and opening them up. Some of them are full of money. Ten million, five million. Some of them are empty. That's this machine," I said. Celal and Irfan were standing next to me. They were staring in astonishment at the gambling machine with its gold and fish.

Irfan said, "What a strange thing! I can't take my eyes off it. It's been put in between the other grave stones like another grave stone," he said.

Celal was transfixed by the machine.

"I've never seen anything like it. Hey, would you tell us what you just told us, again . . . What's this machine called?" he said.

"Marine," I said.

"What kind of machine is it?"

"It's a gambling machine, a slot machine. Japanese make, the latest model electronic machine."

"It's really attractive," murmured Celal.

"Who knows how many engineers worked to make it attractive," I said.

"Look," Irfan cried out in excitement. "There's a bowl next to the machine with money in it!"

"They're chips," I said.

"They left chips so you can play the machine," Celal was saying. "How do you play it? Let me give it a try."

"Take five chips. Put them in that slot. Fine. Now push that button."

When Celal pushed the button, the machine began to work. The sea creatures on the screen flipped by and then stopped.

Four bags of gold had come up. They began to whirl around. Celal shouted out with an excitement I cannot describe.

"Four gold! I got four gold ones at once! They're whipping around! Now what do I do?"

"Great luck," I said. "You pick one of the gold bags and open it. Look, you push on that button there."

"Man, I have to find the one with the gold in it!" said Celal. "I wonder which button I should press . . . One or three, or another one?"

Irfan said with a low voice next to me, "'Tell me about life,' he said to you. Well, in one minute he caught up to life," he said.

⤳•

"We're here," said Gül Abla. "Adviye Hanım lives here. Take this package of Turkish Delight so I can get out of the car easily."

"Let me help you, Gül Abla."

"Okay. We go up to the second floor. You give Adviye Hanım the Turkish Delight."

We went together into an old Ankara apartment building. I looked at the name. It was the "Hayat Apartments." Like all the old Ankara apartments, it was painted in a kind of greenish color. The windows visible from outside weren't very wide, and the building had the kind of recessed balconies I loved. The interiors of these apartments were dark, as though they were holding on, protecting an old world. There were flowers in the window. Beefsteak begonias, regular begonias, lilies, and old-fashioned forgotten things you hardly saw anymore.

I was very excited. My heart was beating as though it were about to burst. I was just about to see Adviye.

Adviye . . . I wondered how the years had treated her.

Gül Abla rang the bell on the second floor. I was trembling, with the package of Turkish Delight in my hand.

The door opened.

Adviye was standing in front of me.

When I saw her, I was taken aback at first. She must have been in her fifties. She had a unique beauty, an unapproachable powerful mysteriousness. She didn't look her age. She had gathered her hair back on her neck. She was wearing a dress the color of pale pomegranate flowers. Her black eyes were deep and sensitive.

In one second she had taken me under her influence.

She met us smiling.

"Come in, welcome. Please come inside. Gül Hanım, I'm so happy to see you," she said. She shook my hand as well. "Welcome," she said.

We went into a semi-dark, nicely decorated living room. The sconces on the wall were lit. I sat in the armchair in the corner.

"I made hot tea for you," Adviye Hanım said. "I made an apricot tart. I don't know if it's any good. My oven isn't that good. Would you like a cigarette?"

I took a cigarette out of the silver box she held out to me.

I looked around with interest. There were some photographs on end tables. One of them was a white-haired elderly man. This must be the judge. He had a stern look, hardly smiling. In another corner I saw the photo of a young girl and young man. They had their arms around each other and were smiling.

Adviye Hanım said, "My daughter and my son. My son is studying abroad now. The girl's still around here. If she comes, you can meet her."

She brought our teas. I was smoking my cigarette and sipping at my tea.

I watched Adviye Hanım as she went in and out of the kitchen. Her body was quite thin, her legs flawless. Gül Abla, as though she read my thoughts, said:

"Really, bless you, you haven't aged at all, you know. You're still like a young girl."

Adviye Hanım laughed sweetly.

"Oh my dear Gül Hanım . . . you just see things as beautiful. Where's beauty now . . . we've been around over half a century," she said.

She sat down across from me and crossed her legs. Taking a sip from her tea, she looked at me.

"I knew Adviye as a young girl," said Gül Abla. "She was a knockout. When she went for a walk around here, all of Yenişehir went wild. If you had any idea how many were after her . . . Ah, Adviye, ah!"

Adviye Hanım was laughing.

"Please, Gül Hanım, your friend is going to think something was going on. No, my dear, I was just a regular young girl, that's all!"

"No, no," said Gül Abla. "I know Adviye, I know everything. One young man fell for you and threw himself out the window. All Ankara heard about it. He was a surgeon's son, I think. . . . It was long ago, I can't remember exactly now. People talked about this dark love for months, the newspapers ran headlines about the tragic event."

Adviye Hanım's color suddenly went pale, her sensitive black eyes saddened.

"Celal," she said. "That was such a painful thing. Poor Celal. For years he would come before my eyes before I went to sleep. He was young. Younger than me. Probably twenty years old. He must have been full of emotion. It was such a painful event, why did you think of this now, Gül Hanım?" she said.

Gül Abla said, "I don't know. I upset you, Adviye. I wanted to say how beautiful you were. Suddenly poor Celal came out," she said.

Adviye Hanım said, looking at me: "We're boring our guest with these old memories. These things she hasn't heard and doesn't know about. Things that are stuck in the dust of the past."

"I'm not bored at all, I'm interested," I said. "I don't want to upset you, but I'm curious about this Celal. . . ."

"As I said, he was very young," said Adviye Hanım. Her eyes drifted off.

"He saw me in a dentist's waiting room. But you know how it is when you're young, I was in love with somebody else. You know those years . . . Then that painful thing happened. At night he would pass in front of my house and look at my window. One day I told him not to do that anymore, that I loved someone else. We were sitting together in the Özen Patisserie on the Boulevard. I didn't know he was going to do something like this. I remember that moment as if it were now. Something gleamed in his eye and then died. I can't forget that moment. Then I got up and left the patisserie. That night. That night he threw himself from his bedroom window. I blamed myself for years." Her voice was trembling. Tears started to flow from her eyes.

Adviye Hanım was weeping.

"I've upset you!" I exclaimed. "Why did we talk about these things? You've become upset."

Gül Abla said to me, "Occasionally she talks about it. She tells what happened and relaxes. She's always struggling with that event in her past. Leave her, let her cry, it's good for her."

Adviye Hanım was softly crying, drying her eyes with a little handkerchief she had crushed in her palm.

"Poor Celal, poor Celal," she kept saying.

"Let her cry, it's good for her," said Gül Abla. She took a sip of her tea.

The doorbell rang.

Adviye Hanım got up from her place and opened the door.

"It's Filiz, Filiz is here," she said. "Filiz, we have guests. Let me introduce you."

A young girl came into the room. This must be what Adviye Hanım was like in her youth, I figured. She looked very much like her mother, a young girl with jet black hair and fine white skin. She came and shook my hand.

"Mommy, are you crying again? Wait, let me get your medicine," she said.

Gül Abla said, "Those old things again. She told us about them and began to cry," she said.

"Her nerves keep getting worse. She has to take her pills regularly, but she doesn't, probably," said the girl. "Mom, what's happened this time? I'm bringing the medicine. Come on, tell me what happened."

"Celal," said Adviye Hanım. "I thought of Celal."

"Oh Mom, you keep on doing this. Look, I brought you some water as well. Take both of those medicines. Now you'll calm down. Leave off getting upset about that Celal. What did the doctor tell you, did you forget? You bore no fault in what happened. Just forget about this strange page from the past now."

"I am guilty, I know. I am guilty." said Adviye Hanım, drowning in sobs.

I didn't know what to do. I lit another cigarette.

"Let's go. Without wanting to, we've upset your mother," I said to Filiz. "I'm very sorry this happened."

"No, really. Please sit down. My mother's been like this for years. This has nothing to do with you. She suddenly remembers those days from the past and she begins to cry. In a little while she'll relax and stop crying. Let me bring you some fresh tea," she said

Adviye Hanım had gone over to a dark corner of the salon now. She was someplace in her own world.

※

Celal pressed button number two. "He found the full one!" shouted Irfan. "The one that's full and has 100 written on it."

The screen flashed, and now rows and rows of new gold bags appeared. They were quivering, dancing about together like anchovies in a rough sea.

"They're here again!" said Celal excitedly. "Which one do you think I should press?"

"Three, press three!" said Irfan.

Celal pressed button number three, and the gold bags began to open one by one. Number three bag turned out empty. The bags of gold were erased from the gleaming screen. Now crabs, swordfish, and starfish began to flash by again.

"I lost. But no problem. This is incredible. What is this, what did you call it?" asked Celal.

"Gambling," I said. "This is gambling."

Irfan said, "It's very exciting. You can't take your eyes off of it."

<hr />

We were sitting across from one another in Gül Abla's little flower-filled room. She took a look at her African violets and plucked off one or two yellow leaves.

"I saw Adviye Hanım," I said thoughtfully. "It upset me. She's a woman who hasn't been able to eradicate that nightmare inside for years, she's become neurotic. What a beautiful woman. Isn't life strange, Gül Abla?"

Gül Abla had put on her eyeglasses that made her eyes look larger and was staring at me.

"Life is truly strange," she said. "When did you see Adviye Hanım? What you're saying really surprises me . . . Neurotic?"

"Isn't she?" I asked.

"But we haven't gone there yet, I'm getting ready now. We'll go. You still haven't seen her. How can you know what her psychological state is like?" she asked.

I was astonished.

"We went together to Adviye Hanım's house! She had on a pomegranate flower dress. She was so beautiful. When we started to talk about Celal she began to cry. She gave us tea in thin-waisted tea glasses. The two of us were there just a little while ago, Gül Abla . . . ," I said.

"We were there a little while ago? I don't think so. We'll go in a little while," said Gül Abla.

"How can that be!" I cried. "What about what I saw, what I experienced! They were real, real!"

"Were they real, I wonder?" asked Gül Abla with a calm voice. She continued to take the yellow leaves off the African violets.

"Real, everything was real!" I said.

"Well, if that's the way you want it, fine, that's the way it'll be. Anyway, what is true, what is not, is it clear?" she said. "If you say, 'I saw something real, I experienced something real,' what can I say? All right, let me put on my fur. The package of Turkish Delight is there on the sideboard. Call a taxi and let's go," she said.

I lifted up the cover on the old black telephone on the side table and dialed the number of the taxi stand.

I was distracted by thought in the taxi. I didn't even see the streets as we twisted and turned through them.

"What's the matter with you?"

"Nothing, I was just thinking."

"You're thinking of him."

"Yes."

"Have you heard anything?"

"Not yet."

"You'll hear something. Wait."

"I'm doing that, anyway."

Inside the taxi on the way to Adviye Hanım's with Gül Abla, I suddenly thought of Bartın. Bartın was so beautiful.

A unique unspoiled Black Sea city . . . but very lively. She had told me about Bartin, where she lived as a young person while on assignment. I wanted to go and see it. I arrived in Bartin one day in the afternoon.

I set out that day from a very hot Ankara and arrived in a humid and cloudy Bartin. I was filled with her. I felt as though I was sharing every step with her as I walked through the narrow old streets of Bartin. The old houses of the little city immediately captured my interest. In the center there was a big main avenue, and on one side a massive fountain. The whole day I walked through streets where she had once walked; maybe I even sat in the tea garden where she had sat in the evenings. Within two hours I got to know Bartin very well. I learned about Bartin Creek, which flows softly in the shadow of the willows; the little market square, where there are a number of shops; the series of embankments that spread down the bluff from the hospital. I sat in the Çınar tea garden across from the bus station drinking a sweet coffee and breathing in the humid air, thinking of her the whole day long.

In the main avenue an old building caught my eye that had muddy paint thrown on it. There were piles of old crooked signs that over time had been forgotten piled against it. The building said "Taşhan" on it. I parked the car next to the fountain and crossed the street and went right inside the door of the Taşhan. I came into a dilapidated old courtyard. There were no women around. Defeated looking men had pulled up chairs to makeshift tables and were drinking and smoking; some of them were playing cards. In the center of the courtyard was a dried up fountain. That's how I remember it. You could see the abandoned half-collapsed upper floors of the Taşhan with their balconies. There was the clicking of backgammon tiles, and occasionally the sigh of a drunkard.

I left the Taşhan and went to the bathroom in the Balkaya Patisserie across the way, then had a profiterole and cold lemonade.

This environment had affected me. There were no women there, but I understood that it was "the beer hall for men who bore women in their hearts." Every man that I saw there was certain to have a woman in his brain, in his heart, and on his lips; these women were unseen, but they were there, in the sound of the backgammon and in the foam on the beer. Maybe some of them were stark naked, just sitting there, soft and warm. Some of them were as silent as photographs with their shadowy faces, some of them were happy, some of them were sad.

I was sitting there thinking of this female presence I had sensed in the Taşhan. Drunken heads recall women differently. . . . All of them are beautiful, sexy, their hair waves around on their neck when they laugh, they have full lips meant for kissing, their eyes are languid and amorous.

Bartin had touched me. There must be traces of her here, I had to find them. I wondered what kind of house she lived in, when she went to work in the evening, what roads she took, did the slowly flowing Bartin Creek ever catch her eye, what did she think?

When she came to me I asked her.

"What streets did you live on in Bartin; I forgot to ask you when I was going. . . ."

It was a place near the Hospital Hill, Asmalı Street. She was happy. Her eyes were looking at my eyes. I offered her blackberries, coffee, and black grapes.

The excited way I told her about Bartin got her excited as well.

"Could you see the Bartin Creek from your house?"

"Yes, my windows looked at the Bartin Creek," she said.

After Bartin I went over to Amasra and I was completely overcome by the unspoiled beauty of this area where blue and green mixed together.

"Have your meal in the Canlı Balık restaurant. Order their special salad. Have them put vinegar on it instead of lemon."

As I sat in the Canlı Balık restaurant, eating the fried white-fish and a salad made of very unusual herbs, greens, tomatoes, cucumber, and pickles, I looked out at one of the bright blue bays lying in front of me, and took many photographs to show her.

We looked at the pictures together in her house.

"Next time, let's go there together," she said.

"All right. We can look through the Taşhan together."

She laughed.

"The Taşhan. You saw that right away, didn't you?"

"How could I not? Did you ever sit in the Taşhan?"

"I sat there a few times and had a beer. It's an old building left over from the Italians . . . Did you see the Italian market?"

"I didn't. I couldn't find it."

"But I told you where it was."

"There's no place like that there anymore. I asked a lot of people, no one knew."

"And the fountain?"

"I saw the fountain. I found a store, near the fountain in a side street, that sold block prints. Sweet, friendly young girls lifted down the rolls of prints from the shelves and spread them on the counter in front of me. I really liked that kerosene smell they have in that humid Bartin air. When I looked at those black, pink, white, purple prints with their branches and roses, I felt like I was walking through gardens I had never seen before. You were in the gardens, and I was picking the flowers from the block prints and giving them to you." I said.

She was shelling nuts for me.

"Did you find the streets in Amasra where they sell the wood handicrafts?"

"Yes, I did. There were very beautiful wooden ships. I got some for myself. A straw bag, a dried crab. . . . Look, I put them over there."

She carefully picked up the dried crab from the table and sniffed it.

"It's still not dry."

"Leave it there. When the heat comes on, it will dry," I said. "I bought it from an old man. He picked out the nicest one for me. Look, this necklace I'm wearing is made out of pine cones. The old man makes these with his own hands."

She looked at my necklace. "What a beautiful thing this is," she said.

I was wandering through Bartin all over again. I was seeking out the traces of the past she had left behind her here ten years ago. Perhaps when she had a headache, she would go into one of those pharmacies on the hospital hill and get some medicine. She certainly sat in the Çınar tea garden. She gazed at the Bartin Creek as it slowly flowed by. She asked for a soft drink, maybe for a freshly brewed tea.

"You just drifted off," said Gül Abla. The taxi shook and came to a halt.

"We're here. Let's get out. You'll hear, don't worry," she said.

"I'm guilty too, Gül Abla."

"I know."

"I sent him a letter."

"When?"

"Two days ago. He got it."

"What did you write in the letter?"

"That I loved him."

"I told you you'd hear. Just wait a little."

We got out of taxi and went into an old Ankara Apartments painted green with recessed balconies.

≫₀

Irfan the Paradise guard was at my side. He said, "He's caught up in that machine. He can't pull himself away. Is he winning anything, I wonder?" indicating Celal.

Celal was throwing the chips in the slot by fives, pushing the buttons with great professionalism and stopping the machine. He had learned how to play quite well.

"He's winning," I said. "Look, he got six gold counts. He won six million."

"Now three gold ones may come," said Celal. "Just now three blue fish and a red starfish came. Two hundred count. I could have added more to it, but I said forget it. It could have gone on. Look! Three gold ones came, see!"

Three gold ones came, flipping over and over.

"There's a lot more money under the three. Be careful Celal," I said. "If you can get onto the second round, there'll be bigger numbers."

"I'm pushing the first gold," he said.

We watched him in excitement. The first gold turned out full.

"Two hundred," said Celal.

"Now the second round is starting."

"I think I should play three this time."

"Maybe you should push the last gold . . . ," said Irfan.

Celal pressed three.

"I got the full one!"

Irfan muttered, "Lucky . . . lucky in gambling."

"The machine's still on. Keep going. Stop it when it starts to eat them," I said.

"Maybe I'll get four swordfish," said Celal.

"What does that make?"

"Jackpot! I get two hundred million!" He continued to play the machine that was shooting out light in the darkness of the night.

"I found Adviye," I said into his ear.

He stopped for a minute. He took his fingers away from the button of the machine.

"Did you find Adviye?" he asked in excitement.

"Yes. I found her. I saw her, talked to her. I know her house."

"Let me just finish this game and we'll talk," said Celal.

Irfan said, "The machine has hypnotized him. Look, he can't pull himself away."

"Yes," I said. "These latest model Japanese machines are like that. A person just can't leave them."

"Adviye is an old story," I said. "But this machine is a new thing for him."

"I'd like to play too," said Irfan.

"We'll go to the Casino Venus," I said. "You can play there."

"The Casino Venus?"

It's a gambling house. A magic world. A unique place."

"Do you think they'd let me in there?" asked Irfan.

"Why shouldn't they?"

"I'm a civil servant. You know, the Paradise guard. . . ."

"Do you have it written on your face?" I asked. "You can get in. Everybody gets in."

"I read in the newspapers. . . ."

"But the Casino Venus is different . . . ," I said.

"How is it different?"

"It's very different. When you get there, you'll see."

"God damn it! Three swordfish came! The fourth slipped by, I missed it!" said Celal.

"Casino Venus . . ." muttered Irfan. "What an unusual name . . . I'll never forget it. Casino Venus."

⇒₀

Nighttime. There was a half moon. It went in and out of the mist.

I went into the Taşhan.

It was just the way I had last left it. As though the same men were sitting at the same tables, playing cards and backgammon, drinking *rakı* and occasionally sighing. I walked around the fountain in the middle whose water had dried up, and went to the back of the courtyard.

Nobody had noticed that I had come in. It must have been almost morning. Outside, Bartin had gone into a deep and dreamless sleep. The lights in the windows had gone out, the streets were completely empty.

I sat down next to an empty table in the very back. The waiter was passing by me, but he didn't even raise his head and look at me.

"Waiter, over here!" I called.

He didn't hear me.

A man sitting at the next table with sunken cheeks who was drinking *rakı* heard me.

"The waiter didn't hear you, right?"

"No, he didn't. They're very preoccupied. Actually, I was going to order a beer," I said.

"He won't hear you," said the man. He lit a cigarette from a half-empty pack and held out the pack to me.

"Thanks," I said. I took a cigarette from the pack. The man leaned over a little and lit my cigarette with an old lighter that smelled of gasoline.

"Why won't the waiter hear me?"

"He won't hear or see. I mean, he won't pay any attention," the man said.

"But why?" I asked.

"He thought that you were one of the women in the heads of all these guys here, that's why."

What I heard astonished me.

"He thought I was one of the women in the heads of these men here?"

"Yes."

"Is that really possible? I felt too that there were women in the hearts and minds of the men here, but how does the waiter know this?"

"The waiter knows those women," said the man. He took a deep drag from his cigarette and a mouthful from his *rakı*.

I could hear the sounds from the tiles of the men around me playing backgammon.

"Does the waiter know the women in the hearts and minds of the men here?"

"He knows them. He knows all of them."

"How can that be?"

"Those women come here, and sit at the tables. The waiter knows them," he said.

He was staring straight at me.

"Well, are these women real? How can they come here?" I asked.

"Since they're being thought about, they're real, of course," said the man. "But they're illusionary women. You know . . . caught in the men's dreams, stuck in a corner of the heart, turned into a whisper on the lips, lost in the depths of the past, madly loved, women who were finally found or who could never be gotten to. You know, illusionary women."

"When do they come here?" I asked with interest.

"In a little while."

"At what time?"

"They come when the moon sets. In a little while."

"Will I be able to see them?"

"You'll see them, why shouldn't you see them?" he said. "If you look carefully, you'll see them, those women."

I was excited.

"So, illusionary women," I said.

"Yes, illusionary women," he said.

The door of the Taşhan opened with a little scraping. I turned in that direction. A woman entered through the open door. This was a young woman, whose long brown hair hung down around her shoulders. She was looking around. As though she were trying to check out who was in the Taşhan.

"Makbule's here," said the man next to me.

"Makbule?"

"Yes."

"Do you know her?"

"I used to know her. The girl Hüseyin used to be in love with."

Makbule slipped between the tables and went over to the table of a dark man who was sitting near us, pulled up a chair, and sat down.

"She sat at Hüseyin's table," said the man. He lit another cigarette.

Hüseyin, who had been sitting quietly until then, suddenly came alive. He was talking to the woman in a voice we couldn't hear.

"Hüseyin and Makbule . . . ," I said.

"Yes," said the man. "Years ago, Hüseyin was crazy in love with Makbule. They'd meet in secret, get together in tea gardens and talk and look at Bartin Creek flowing by. They were in love with one another. Hüseyin was working at the market in the square. He wanted to kidnap the girl. They wouldn't let her marry him. Then all of a sudden they married Makbule off to a rich factory owner. Now she lives in Bartın's richest house. The old factory owner bought a summer place in Amasra as well. They had kids. So, life goes on. . . . Hüseyin comes to the Taşhan every night. He waits for Makbule. And, as you saw, Makbule came," he said.

"Incredible!" I said in excitement. "You mean she runs out of the house every night and comes here. . . ."

The man chuckled.

"She doesn't run out of the house. She's next to her husband, sleeping in bed."

"But Makbule is here now, sitting across from Hüseyin."

"Yes, to be in the place she wants. The place where she's wanted, loved, thought about. Across from her lover," said the man.

"The moon must have gone down outside."

"Yes, the moon set."

"Makbule is real," I said. "Not like an illusion. A woman of flesh and blood."

"In one way, that's true," muttered the man.

"How can this be, I don't get it . . . ," I said.

"These things aren't very clear anyway," said the man.

Another woman slipped in through the door of the Taşhan.

"İffet," said the man.

"İffet?"

"İffet."

İffet's hair was tousled, she was looking fearfully into the fastnesses of the Taşhan.

"She saw Kemal," said the man.

I looked where he pointed. There was a huge man with a moustache sitting at the table. When he saw İffet, he sat up slightly in his chair. İffet passed quickly through the tables and went straight over to him. She virtually collapsed into the chair he pulled out for her. She seemed beat. A little sweaty. I could see her face in the low light of the Taşhan. Her hands with their long white fingers were trembling. She lit a cigarette. Kemal leaned over to her and was telling her something.

"Poor İffet . . . ," said the man. He sighed.

"İffet seems excited and exhausted."

"Yes, Kemal stabbed her to death two years ago."

"Kemal stabbed her to death!"

"Yes. It was a crime of love and jealousy. Things like that happen. One Saturday he stabbed the woman he was crazy in love with over by the fountain. He stopped her and asked her something. Then he . . ."

"Did İffet love him?"

"She was crazy about him, how could she not be. . . . Jealousy, that's all!

"Kemal was inside for years. After he got out he came every night to the Taşhan. For a while he sat all alone at his table. He was lost in his own world, his own pains, and his own darkness. Then one night İffet came. The moon had set. The door opened a little. We saw İffet. It was an incredible moment. Those of us who knew the story were amazed. We listened all night long as they sat at that table talking and looking into one another's eyes. Kemal kept holding her hands. Like he never wanted to let them go again. İffet came. She finally came. After that night Kemal changed a lot. We saw a glint of hope in his eyes, a strange, soft look. It was love. We realized that. İffet comes every night and they sit and talk like this."

The things I had experienced in the Taşhan left me in amazement.

Through the half-opened door of the Taşhan different women slowly came in, looked and found their men sitting at the tables, and went over and sat down across from them.

Whispered conversations and occasional single words floated through the air.

"Look, Melike!" said the man. I turned and looked. The woman coming in was very beautiful. She had dark-colored shining eyes, bright blonde hair and a delicate mouth. She was tall, thin, and graceful. She had on a sparkling sequined dress in an unusual color. Her long eyelashes shadowed her cheeks, as she perused the interior of the Taşhan with her beautiful eyes.

"Melike . . . The nightclub's most beautiful woman. A number of guys are in love with her. Let's see, who will she sit with tonight?"

"Does she sit at a different table every night?"

"Yes, she sits at a different table every night."

Melike sauntered over towards the table of the man who was talking to me. Her eyes stopped at me for a minute. She carefully checked me out. She came and sat at the man's table.

The man was excited. His colorless face filled with color, and his eyes seemed to glow.

Looking straight at me, Melike said in a sexy voice, "Oh, you good-for-nothing, you just forgot all about me." Her voice was low and steamy.

"I didn't forget you, Melike, how could I forget?" said the man.

He could hardly speak for excitement, his eyes were glowing like coals.

"That night . . . You didn't forget, did you, that night?" asked Melike.

The man: "Maybe the only night I remember from my whole life up to now is that night, Melike."

"Get me a whiskey," said Melike. She took the man's hands in her palms.

The man was overcome for an instant.

"I've never had another night like that Melike . . . ," he murmured. "After that night, I realized that so much of my life had just been completely empty."

A glass of whiskey came to the table. Melike lifted her glass, "To that night!" she said. She drank down half the whiskey. "How are your wife and kids?"

"How should they be? Everything's the same. We go on living . . . ," said the man. His voice had grown sad.

"Don't be sad . . . I like you when you're happy," said the woman. She stroked the man's cheek with her long fingers.

When the woman's hands touched this worn out man, aged by time, he came alive, young again, his sagging body became erect.

I watched the transformation with interest.

"Did you feel guilty afterwards?" asked Melike.

"No," said the man. He thought for a bit. "I wanted to leave my home. I just wanted to be with you. There was a strange storm inside me. . . ."

"Really," said Melike. "Now you're here every night, aren't you?"

"Yes, I come every night to the Taşhan. I sit here and wait for the moon to set."

Melike took a mirror out of her little velvet bag and took a look at her face.

"The moon set a long time ago."

"Is it cool outside?"

"Very cool."

"Aren't you cold? Your clothes are thin."

"They left me off with the car," said Melike.

"Who left you?"

"It's not important."

"Okay."

The Taşhan had now become quite crowded. The tables were full, the conversations were picking up. The waiters were moving about among the tables, giving out food and drink.

I slowly got up from my place and went outside. I wandered around a little in Bartin's streets without people. The tea gardens had closed, all the lights were off.

I walked for a while in the dark night. I came back to the Taşhan. I pushed the heavy door a little and went inside. Everything was quiet. The men were sitting by themselves. Their eyes were distracted. They had gone back, and seemed to have grown a little older.

The waiter was collecting the plates and glasses. The games with tiles had stopped, the decks of cards were gone.

My man was sitting by himself at his table. I went over to him.

"Where are the illusionary ladies, have they left?" I asked.

"They're gone," he said.

"They didn't stay very long."

"They don't stay long, they leave."

"Tomorrow night. . . ."

"Tomorrow night, when the moon goes down, they'll all come here again."

"If I come here tomorrow night, will you be here?" I asked.

"I'll be here. I'm here every night," said the man. He sighed. "Melike had a new perfume on. . . ."

"A new perfume?"

"Yes. It wasn't the perfume from that night. It was something new."

"Did you ask the name?"

"I asked. It's Organza."

"What a beautiful name," I murmured. "Organza. . . ."

"It suits her," said the man.

Kemal, at the next table, said, "Oof."

The little tea service stuck in a corner of the Taşhan started work. The waiter was now distributing the first morning teas to the tables. He gave me a glass of tea. I took a sip from my tea.

⬎

Celal said, "The machine's starting to eat everything up."

Irfan asked, "No gold has come up in the last nine rounds. Those blue fish aren't coming either. The numbers have really begun to fall. The machine's very quick. What do you think we should do?"

I gave a glance at the machine. It had stopped. It wasn't doing anything. Celal was pushing the buttons, throwing in a chip and waiting impatiently for the gold bags to appear.

"Don't play. Let it go for a while," I said. "The machine's taking it back now. It'll finish up everything in a minute."

"Should we change hands? What if I play a little?" Irfan asked.

"Go ahead and play," said Celal. "It's not giving anything. Play until the credit is finished up. Maybe it'll open up."

"Are these machines all like this?" asked Irfan.

"They're all like this," I said. "After a while they take back everything they give. You have to know when to get up."

"You can't stop playing these things . . . ," said Celal. "What if it gives out something. What if the gold comes again?"

Irfan was sitting down at the machine. He played differently, he didn't put the chips in five at a time but by threes.

"Casino Venus . . . ," he murmured. "I didn't forget it. We're going to go there, right?"

"We will," I said.

⬎

I was in Bartin. I was walking around the streets in the middle of the night, waiting for the time to pass. Just ahead of me, the

Taşhan, on the corner, with its closed door, was pulling me towards itself like a magnet. I walked for a while past the shops with their drawn down shutters, I looked at the fountain standing dark and quiet in the night. I walked towards the hospital hill. I looked at the dark valley down below for a while. With quick steps I walked back to the Taşhan.

There was a woman standing in front of the door. She was obviously chilled by the dampness in the air, standing there with her trench coat wrapped tightly around her. I went over to her.

"Aren't you going inside?" I asked.

"I can't go in," she said. Her voice was depressed. She looked at me in despair.

"Let's push the door and go in," I said.

"I can't. I can't go in," she said. "Because he doesn't think of me anymore. He's stopped thinking about me. I'm not in his heart, his mind, or his thoughts anymore. It's impossible for me to go in. It's terrible. You understand, don't you?"

"I think I do. But how did this just suddenly happen? How did you disappear from his heart and mind? Is he inside?" I asked.

"He's in there," said the woman. "He's sitting at his regular table."

"Come on, let's go in together," I said.

The woman got panicky.

"No, No," she said. "He won't even see me. I can't do it. I'm not in his thoughts any more, don't you understand."

"Well, what happened?"

"He just erased me from his mind and threw me out."

"Is that easy?" I asked.

"He met some other woman," said the woman. Her voice was full of pain.

"How do you know?"

"I couldn't get in last night either. I waited around here."

"Who is this guy?" I asked.

"Mahmut," she said. "Dark, with a moustache. Mahmut, who was crazy in love with me."

"Where did you hear about the other woman?"

"He told his friend. 'I'm free of the past, free from Mebrure at last,' he said."

"How many days has this been going on?"

"It's been fifteen days. I didn't know what to do. I can't go inside anymore. I can't get to him. I'm at a loss. Time's going by very quickly."

"What kind of relationship did you have?"

The woman looked off into the distance for a minute.

"A deep love that lasted for years," she said.

"What happened?"

"We could never get together. It was mad desire. To be together with one another. You know. . . ."

"Weren't you ever able to get together?"

"Three times. Three nights . . . ," said Mebrure. Her voice was trembling. "He never forgot those three nights. Those three nights that ran into one another like a strange dream. He never forgot them for years. How could something like that happen now? I just can't believe it.

"But," said the woman hopelessly, "as long as he doesn't think of me I can't do anything! I only exist when I'm in his mind."

I was thinking.

"If you wrote him a letter . . ."

"Would it do any good?"

"It might. He might start to think of you again."

"How would we get the letter to him?"

"I'll take it and give it to him."

"I'll write him a letter," said Mebrure. "I have to get paper and pen, and an envelope."

"It's night, all the shops are closed. There's nobody out. It's so quiet in Bartin," I said.

"Everyone's asleep," she said. She was searching through her bag, looking for a pen.

There was an echoing sound in the empty street of someone's high heels. The two of us saw at the same instant that a woman was approaching the Taşhan.

"That's her, that's the woman! The one Mahmut is thinking about now. The woman who's in his heart and his mind!" said Mebrure.

"How do you know that she's the woman?"

"I know. She's a widow. They met in the tea garden."

I looked at the woman. She had class, and she was nice. Her hair was blown up like a lion's mane. She pushed open the door of the Taşhan confidently and went inside.

Mebrure was standing next to me, trembling.

"She's there, she's there next to him. She went inside . . . ," she said.

"You prepare the letter, I'll take it and give it to him," I said. "Write the letter. I'm going inside now. When the woman leaves I'll give him your letter."

"What should I say?" asked Mebrure.

"That you love him. . . ."

❧

I pushed open the door of the Taşhan and went inside. I saw Mahmut right away. He was sitting at a table near the door. As Mebrure said, he had a moustache and was swarthy. The woman was sitting next to him; they were hand in hand. A waiter brought a plate of fruit and placed it on the table.

I took a look around. The man I always spoke to was sitting at the table next to me. İffet had come. She was sitting across from Kemal. They weren't talking, just staring at one another.

At the tables at the edge, one or two women I hadn't seen before caught my eye. I sat down at the table where I had sat the night before.

"You're late tonight," the man said.

"I was talking with someone outside."

"Mahmut and the new woman he's fallen in love with," he said; he showed me the table where Mahmut was sitting.

"Does Mahmut fall in love often?" I asked.

The man shook his head.

"No. For years he loved the same woman with a dark love. Mebrure. He couldn't see anyone but her. She used to come here every night, Mebrure. They were lovers who could never get together, you know what I mean, a dark love. . . . Suddenly fifteen days ago he met this woman and everything changed."

"Who is this woman?"

"She's a widowed nurse. She was just assigned to Bartın. Take a look, she's a nice lady, she's got taste. Vibrant, full of life. She's driven Mahmut nuts. Now she comes here every night. You know what it's like when a relationship is just new . . . ," he said. His dull eyes lit up for a minute.

"His old lover is waiting outside the door. She's in pain, hopeless. She can't come inside. I was talking to her just a minute ago," I said.

"Poor Mebrure," said the man. He took a sip of his *rakı*. "She's condemned to become a shadow in the past now."

"You think so?"

"That's what I think. Look at them . . ." Saying this, he pointed to Mahmut's table.

Mahmut and the woman were wrapped in an embrace. In the dim light of the Taşhan you wouldn't notice unless you looked closely. The woman's full white breasts were spilling out of her black silk blouse. I could see the strap of her bra. Her plump knees were pressed against Mahmut's under the table.

"Sexual attraction . . . ," murmured the man. "Everything starts with that. Something that happens in an instant. Like an electric current. When you touch it, it spreads to everything and you burn up. There's nothing you can do."

"Things like this sometimes burn out quickly," I said.

"Who knows . . . ," said the man.

"What's the woman's name?"

"Meral."

~≫•

"You're very distracted today," said Gül Abla. "You were in the Casino Venus, weren't you? You went there again. You can't not go. Well, anyway, it's a colorful place. The machines captivate you.

"Yes," I said. "I was in the Casino Venus."

I was distracted. My eyes were tired. I had been playing the machines for six hours without a break.

"Your eye is bloodshot, your left eye," said Gül Abla.

"I know. I'll put in some drops. The colors and lights in the machine tire my eyes," I said.

"God, what is this machine, anyway . . . ," Gül Abla complained. "Ever since you got involved with that you hardly come to see me."

"It's an incredible thing, this machine," I said.

"It's a machine, that's all, a gambling machine. . . ."

"No," I said. "It's not just a gambling machine."

"What else could it be! Maybe when you play you forget about everything, but an ordinary machine. And you lose money while you're playing it."

"Gül Abla!" I said. "You just don't understand my machine. I have no idea how I can explain it to you. It's as though it's alive. It recognizes me, it feels it when I come and sit down at it. I know this very well. When I start to press the buttons and control it I can feel that it trembles for an instant. It's a male machine. An out-of-the-ordinary, good-for-nothing male. Or maybe a real man. Sometimes he disappoints me, then suddenly makes me happy. He gets annoyed, then he calms down. Sometimes he's strong enough to take everything I own. He makes me feel it. I'm frightened of him then. Then suddenly he gives me everything. But I can never be sure of him. He has something that he's hiding. I can't trust him, do you know what I mean? Somebody who drives a car fast, who likes the night, drinking, and women, sometimes like velvet, sometimes quiet and sullen. . . . He's a real man. . . ."

Gül Abla was listening to me closely.

"It's so strange the way you explained that machine to me. . . . Now you've got me curious," she said. "You explained it as though you were in love with it. A male machine. . . ."

"Love. . . . Not love, passion," I said. "What I was talking about was passion. It's true that I feel a great passion towards it. In order to see it, to be with it, I run over to the Casino Venus. If somebody else is sitting at my machine, I get jealous. I can't sit still. The other machines don't interest me. My eyes are always on that one. If it gives something to someone else, I get tense with anxiety in my seat. I can't wait until it frees up."

"You astonish me," said Gül Abla.

"I don't know. Will I ever get tired of it? It just caught me and made me a prisoner. Sometimes I hate it," I said.

"Well, what is this machine . . . ," said Gül Abla.

"I spend hours alone with it," I said. Face to face. We know one another's signals very well now. I know very well when it's

in a bad mood, the days when it's not going to give me anything. I realize it as soon as I sit down. It's a strange moment.
We look at one another. It's ready there in front of me, with its
unusual colors and the lights on the side. As though it starts
off by talking to me. It starts to make little surprises. I get all
settled in my seat. My cigarettes have come. I ask for a coffee.
I'm caught in that strange attraction now. Sometimes it gives
me a lot of money.

"Sometimes it takes all your money. It's a mechanism built
on deception. That machine's been put there to fool you. Not
to give you money, but to take your money. The whole thing
has been set up to fool you. Don't you understand that?" asked
Gül Abla.

"But it's a game, a two-sided game. Between the machine
and me," I said.

"Other people do the same thing."

"But they don't feel what I feel!" I shouted.

"How do you know?"

"I know, I just know! It's my machine!" I shouted. "You
don't understand me!"

"The Casino Venus," said Gül Abla. "That male machine
of yours. You've become addicted to it. A deception. These are
dangerous things. . . ."

"Yes," I said. "That's why I like them. When I go into the
Casino Venus, when I pass through that locked revolving glass
door, I get a rush of excitement. I know the danger. These are
really dangerous things. Maybe that's why they're so attractive."

᠅

A cold wind had started to blow in the Bartin night. Mebrure
was standing next to me. We were in front of the door of the
Taşhan. The moon had long since set.

"I wrote the letter," she said. She was holding a white envelope in her hand. "I wrote everything to him. All the pain I felt, my feelings that I wanted to see him. . . ."

"Did you seal the envelope?"

"Yes, I did."

"Give it to me. I'll go inside now and give it to Mahmut," I said.

Mebrure suddenly got excited. She was undecided for a moment there in front of the Taşhan's door.

"Should I give it to you? Do you think it's the wrong thing to do?" she asked.

"What's there to lose? Give me the letter. I'm going in," I said.

Mebrure held out the envelope to me.

I pushed open the door of the Taşhan and went into its half-dark world.

My man was sitting at his usual table. He was alone. I looked at Mahmut's table, it was empty. I turned to the man and asked in confusion, "Where did they go?"

"They went up to one of the rooms upstairs," he said.

"When?"

"An hour ago."

"There are rooms upstairs in the *han?*"

"Yes," said the man. "Look, those doors you can see behind the iron banisters."

"How can I get up there?"

"There's a stairs next to the tea kitchen."

Next to the tea kitchen there was a narrow stairs that led upwards. I climbed the worn marble steps. The balcony level of the *han* was filled with rooms whose doors were closed. How strange that I had never noticed them before. I wondered which room Mahmut and Meral were in. I had forgotten to ask the man. There was no one around. I knocked on a random door.

"Who's there?" said a harsh male voice.

"I was looking for Mahmut Bey . . ."

"Mahmut Bey's not here," said the voice.

"Who are you?" I asked timidly.

"I'm the district attorney. I'm resting in this room. Who are you?"

"I brought a letter for Mahmut Bey. It's an emergency. I have to get it to him," I said.

The DA said, "Mahmut's in the next room."

"Thanks."

I knocked on the door of the next room.

"Who are you?" said a male voice.

"I was looking for Mahmut Bey. I brought him an important letter. I have to get it to him tonight. . . ."

The door opened a little. Mahmut stuck his head out of the crack in the door and looked at me. He was wearing an undershirt.

"A letter?"

"Yes, I brought you a letter. Here it is."

He reached out and took the letter. He closed the door. I went downstairs. I sat at the table next to the one where the man was.

"What happened?" he asked. "You look excited."

"I brought a letter to Mahmut."

"A letter?"

"Yes. Mebrure wrote a letter to him. I brought it over and gave it to him. Think he'll read it right away? Or will he put it in his pocket and forget about it?"

"He'll be curious and open it. Take a look at what it says," said the man.

"There's a woman with him, isn't there?"

"Yes, they went upstairs together to the room."

I was trying to think.

"He might not read the letter," I said.

"You can't be sure. If the woman's asleep, he'll read it," said the man. "We'll know."

"Will we know?"

"We'll know."

I was looking around from where I sat. Suddenly someone was forcing the door of the Taşhan. Someone was hitting the door from outside, pushing a little, it opened a little, then closed again.

"He's reading the letter," said the man. "He opened the envelope and he's reading it."

He took a slice of melon.

"How do you know?" I asked in astonishment.

Mebrure's just about to enter his thoughts again. Look, she's trying the door."

The noise from outside the door grew louder. The door seemed as though it would open, then with a huge crash it slammed closed again.

"The struggle . . . ," murmured the man.

"Is he thinking of Mebrure?"

"He suddenly remembered. But he's not thinking of her at the moment; see, Mebrure can't get in. . . . Like I said, Mahmut is in another crisis. Sex, attraction, desire. . . . These are stronger than Mebrure," he said.

"It's a terrible thing! I murmured. "Poor Mebrure. She can't come in. Look how she's trying the door. . . . She can't get into Mahmut's thoughts. . . . The letter must have had some effect. Look, the door's almost open."

The door almost opened all the way, then slammed shut again.

"It's very tough," said the man. "We're looking at a struggle here. While he's full of lust and desire, it's very difficult for a woman from the past to get into his thoughts."

I sat helplessly in my place. There was a huge force battering at the door of the Taşhan.

"She won't make it," I said.

"Maybe she needs some time."

"Time is two-faced. I'm afraid of time. I think time passing is dangerous."

"There's nothing you can do!" said the man. He was slowly sipping his *rakı*. The noises at the door had stopped.

"She couldn't get inside," I said.

I quickly got up and went outside. The night air struck my face. Mebrure was by the door. Her hair was all undone, the buttons on her trench coat had opened, and one or two of them had torn off. She seemed worn out.

"Were you able to give him the letter?" she asked.

"I gave it to him."

"I can't get in. I keep pushing the door, trying it, just when it seems like it's opening a little, it closes again. I feel like I'm drowning, I feel awful."

"A man's brain and his thoughts," I said. "It's hard to be able to get in there again. He may be letting you in just out of spite."

"That's possible. Yes, that is possible," she said in pain.

"Let's wait."

"What else can I do?"

She was in a full sweat. She leaned against the wall of the Taşhan. The dark silent night of Bartin enveloped both of us.

⁂

Come on," I said to Celal. "We're going."

"Where?" he asked with interest. The machine with the gold pieces had stopped paying out and was taking money now. Irfan the Paradise guard had stopped playing and was sitting to one side.

"We're going, come on."

"Where are we going?"

"To Adviye."

Celal's color suddenly turned grey. He was excited. He shuddered as though an electric current had passed through his whole body.

"To Adviye?"

"Yes."

"How did you find her?"

"I just found her."

He murmured: "To find Adviye again after all these years . . . To see her again . . . How can I bear it. . . . My clothes are old, my silk shirt's gone all yellow. . . . My hair, how's my hair?"

"You're perfectly fine," I said. "You're young. Don't forget that. You're much younger than she is."

"Yes," he said. His eyes were dazed, he was lost in the past.

"Let's go that way. I'll show you Adviye."

The three of us were now standing in the empty lot across the street from the Hayat Apartments, where Adviye lived.

"Does she live here?"

"Yes, that one that's lit up is her window," I said.

"She's pulled the curtains closed," he said.

He couldn't take his eyes off the lit window.

"Go in the building. Go up to the second floor. Number 6. Her husband's not here. Ring the bell," I said.

Celal's face was changing color because of his nerves. In a shaky voice he said, "I can't. I won't be able to do it."

"Why? Haven't you waited for thirty years just to see her once? Didn't you always think of this moment?"

"I can't. I can't go in the apartment building. I can't ring the bell on her door . . ." murmured Celal. I don't want her to suddenly see some pale ghost, some dead person from the past in front of her. What will she do? What will she think when she sees me?"

⁂

"Well, you're not dead at all right now. You're alive. Your lungs are full of oxygen. At this moment, the blood in your veins is coursing like a river, and who knows how fast your heart is beating, your spirit and your brain are all mixed up together, and you're struggling with conflicting emotions. You're not dead or anything like it. Is a dead person like this?" I said.

"But she doesn't know that!"

⁂

"She doesn't know these things! How can I explain all of this to her? She'd be horrified. She won't understand. How can someone come back after a gap of thirty years, knock on the door, and just walk into her world . . ."

I thought for a moment.

"Yes, Adviye probably wouldn't understand what happened. I hadn't thought about this side of things at all," I said.

"What do you think we should do . . . ?" Irfan was saying.

A dog started to bark in one corner of the lot.

"The animal sensed that we were here," Irfan murmured. He went off to the side and lit up a cigarette.

"Her lights . . . Her walking behind the sheer curtains . . . Maybe the shadow I see there is her walking . . . Adviye's there. Right in front of me. If I reach out my hands I'll feel her warmth, the scent of jasmine coming from her hair. I have to make myself get used to this little by little," said Celal.

"Are you afraid?" I asked.

"Yes, I'm afraid. I'm very afraid. What if we waited here until morning . . . ?"

"What are you afraid of?"

"Of losing her again."

"Don't be afraid. Go upstairs," I said. "Knock at the door. She'll put out the lights and go to bed soon. Come, on, go up."

Celal couldn't make up his mind. He didn't know what to do. The light beaming from Adviye's windows was pulling him with an unimaginable power, his black eyes were burning like coals.

"I can't go by myself. I don't have the strength."

Irfan said, "She won't see me, Adviye. I don't appear to just anyone. Come on, let's go upstairs together."

Let's go knock at the door together, then," said Celal. He had pulled himself together a little.

"Come on," said Irfan.

The two of them went into the apartment building.

I was intensely excited. I lit a cigarette and started to wait. The evening frost came.

A minute later I saw a shadow run out of the building straight towards me. It was Irfan.

He can't go inside," he said. "He can't bring himself to ring the bell. He's there, frozen in front of the door. He's shaking all over, from nerves."

"Don't leave him alone. Go to him," I said. "It's not easy. He's someone from the past. He can't just go inside all of a sudden. He can't just rip through thirty years and do that in one minute. We have to help him. Go to him."

Irfan ran inside the apartment building and was lost to sight.

❧

Mebrure and I were side by side. We were leaning against the cold wall of the Taşhan, looking at the silent Bartin night.

"I'll try to get inside again," said Mebrure. "I'll push the door wide open. Time's going by. What a terrible thing time is . . . Every second that goes by is working against me. New visions, new events are placing themselves in Mahmut's mind. All of them just wipe me out and throw me away, do you know what I mean, wipe me out and throw me away . . . ," she murmured bitterly.

"Let's both push against the door," I said. "When it opens a little, you slip inside."

The two of us pushed with all our strength against the thick hard door that bore the marks of the Taşhan's long years.

The door didn't even budge.

"What do you think happened?"

"It means he put the letter aside."

"Let's try the door again."

"Okay, another try."

We pushed at the door with all of our strength again.

"No good," said Mebrure in despair. "The door won't open."

"You wait here. I'll go inside. Move over here to the side," I said.

Mebrure moved away from the door.

I pushed the Taşhan's door. It opened easily. I went inside. The door closed noisily behind me.

The man was sitting in his place. He saw that I had come.

"She can't come in, right?" he asked.

"She can't," I said. I collapsed into a chair.

"Wait, let's see," said the man. "Things can change. It's life, you know. Everything can change in an instant."

"I don't know . . ." I replied.

"Mahmut folded up the letter and put it in his pocket, probably," he said.

"That's what I think."

"But he'll read it later."

"You think he'll read it?"

The man laughed bitterly.

"You think he won't? He can read. He'll read it. He's a man. When he's alone he'll read it for sure," he said.

"Let's wait."

"Yeah, the best thing to do is to wait."

I leaned back and started to observe the world inside the Taşhan.

───※───

Irfan came out of the apartment again. He was running over towards me.

"What happened?" I asked anxiously. Didn't I tell you not to leave him alone? He shouldn't be alone there!"

"I went upstairs and he wasn't in front of the door there, Celal," said Irfan. "There was nobody in front of the door. It was empty in front of Number 6. Celal wasn't there."

I was excited.

"That means he went inside. He pushed the bell and went inside . . . ," I said. "He must have suddenly pulled together the courage."

"I wonder whether he went inside or ran away?" asked Irfan. "I'm responsible for him, you know. Do you think maybe he ran away?"

"Where would he go?"

"He'd just dive into life and disappear. I won't be able to find him again. He was my charge."

"If he ran away, I'd see him. I was here the whole time," I said. "And where would he run away to? This was the place he wanted to come, the place he wanted to get to."

"Right . . . What's going on now, I wonder?"

"I have no idea . . ."

"I'm going upstairs again," said Irfan. "I'll go inside."

"Can you do that?"

"I'll go in. It's easy."

"Okay, hurry up. Tell me what's happening. I'll wait here."
Irfan ran off.

My eyes were fixed on the lights in the window. There was
no motion, no change inside.

I lit another cigarette and began to wait.

⇒⊚

I rang the downstairs bell of Gül Abla's apartment. My eyes
were tired, and my head was ringing a little, my hands were
soiled. Gül Abla pushed the button from upstairs and the door
opened. I ran up the stairs. The lights in the stairwell were
shining brightly. Gül Abla's door with its brass doorknocker
was half open, as usual. I pushed lightly on the delicate brass
knocker.

"Come in, come in," said Gül Abla. Then she opened the
door. I was inside. I brushed by the coat rack where her fur
coats were hanging and went into the little room with the
couch where her African violets were. I sat down in my regular
place, the armchair with the wooden arms upholstered in dark-
cherry colored velvet. Gül Abla was across from me, staring at
me closely. Somewhere inside, a clock slowly chimed out some
different kind of time that really meant nothing to me.

"You're coming from the Casino Venus, aren't you?" asked
Gül Abla.

"Yes, I'm coming from the Casino Venus."

"You're tired."

"The machine wore me out."

"Did you play on your male machine?"

"Yes."

"Your hands are dirty. Go in and wash them. There's a
clean towel on the back of the door. Don't throw paper in the
toilet," said Gül Abla.

I went into the little bathroom painted blue and washed my hands. The grey water that ran off my hand wasn't dirt, but dye from the tokens. I threw a glance at the mirror and went back in beside Gül Abla.

"The machine wore you out, used you up. Your hair is undone; your face is all pale. Whatever are you doing there, I have no idea! Did you lose a lot?"

"No, I didn't lose a lot. I really struggled with the machine. I was just stubborn for hours. It annoyed me."

"Why didn't you go to another machine," asked Gül Abla.

"I couldn't. I just couldn't leave it. It was a tough, heartless day; do you know what I mean? When I first sat in front of it, it was fine. Soft. It was giving me little things. I felt in a good mood. I asked for a coffee, lit up a cigarette. It was as though I was sitting with it and was talking about water and the weather, unimportant things. It was acting like it was going to give me something big, sending out little signals to that effect. Red sevens came. I was pleased. It was going well. . . . Just then, the machine toughened up. Well, it's very hard to understand this. Even though I was angry with it, somehow I could get up from in front of it and leave. My eyes were stuck on the blue bars, on the apples I was waiting for. It was showing me the edge, fooling me. Just like a man. I just couldn't pull myself away from its attraction. It promised me a lot of things, but somehow could never bring itself to deliver. At one point I got fed up and just as I was about to leave, it gave me two apples. I was amazed. The figure on the counter on the side suddenly went up. I gave it all my concentration again. My fingers were on the buttons, my eyes on the blue, purple, and red screen. The count the apples gave me melted away in ten minutes. It stopped. As though it had stopped talking to me. I had to make it move, to bring it back to me again. I got another bowl or two of tokens. I couldn't relax. Everything started to go badly. A red seven and a blue bar came up together. That was strange. My eyes were tired, my head was ringing. I had no hope left. I got up from the machine. I was just about to leave the Casino Venus. I was so tired; you know. . . . A young woman sat in my place. She was throwing in the tokens, pulling down the arm. Then something unimaginable took place before my very eyes. Three diamonds were there side by side on the screen! The counter started to increase like crazy. The young woman gave out a scream of delight. The machine gave her the jackpot. . . .

I watched what was going on, leaning against one of the velvet covered walls of the Casino Venus. I was astonished, destroyed. That machine that had given me such a hard time all of a sudden gave some foreign woman a jackpot. Everyone was gathered there.

"I'm amazed," said the woman. "I suddenly saw three diamonds there. Next to one another, in the same row! Bright blue, don't they look great, though?"

They paid her the money in dollars. She put it in her bag and left the Casino Venus.

I sat down at the machine again. I hated it. My insides were like ice. It was a strange feeling. It hadn't given me the diamonds, and just turned them right over to somebody else. I played a little. The machine was tired, emptied out. It wasn't going to give out any presents now. It seemed as though it were completely indifferent to me. The tension between us was over for the day. After I threw the last token in, I got up from there and came to you."

"Just like a man," murmured Gül Abla. "A dangerous man. A cruel man. He fooled you. You were tired and he gave the diamonds to someone else in front of your eyes. Stay away from him."

"I can't."

"Sit down, don't just rush off. Let me make you a coffee."

She went inside to the kitchen.

My eyes went over to the African violets. Their colors were so beautiful. The purples were multiflora; the pinks had opened like little roses. Gül Abla's green worry beads were waiting, curled in the middle of the table like a little water snake. The clock was now striking some longer period of time. Its sounds were echoing in my groggy head.

≫•

I threw my cigarette off to a corner of the lot. I looked up to see that Irfan had come out of the apartment building and was running towards me.

"What happened? Were you able to get inside?" I asked.

"I just couldn't get inside. I wore myself out trying the door and the wall around it. It's so strange; they must have some unusual verse from the Koran hanging in the house. I couldn't get through the door or the wall. . . . Like I said, there must be a verse somewhere inside protecting the house. When you add something to these verses, people like us can't get inside. You can't get in through the door, or the wall. Good or bad, it doesn't matter; do you know what I mean? Bad luck! And Celal is nowhere around. If I lose him, that's the end of my job. I took him out under my charge. How was I supposed to know he was going to go missing like this . . . ," he said.

He was upset. He sighed deeply.

"He's not lost, he must have gone inside. Nothing's going to happen," I said.

"I don't know. I just can't get inside. He was standing there shaking in front of the door. How could he find the strength to get inside all by himself, I wonder?" he grumbled.

"Come, let's go sit on that wall," I said. We sat down together on the low concrete wall on the side of the lot.

Irfan suddenly poked me.

"Look, look, the light in those windows went out," he said. I looked, and the light in the middle windows went out.
"What's going on?"
"I don't know. . . ."
"Let's wait."

≫●

I had put on my black high-heeled shoes, and put on my fur. I tucked my taxi money in a corner of my little suede purse. I took a last look in the mirror, touched up my lashes and freshened my lipstick.

The taxi had come. I pulled the door shut and went downstairs. I gathered the wide skirts of my fur and got into the taxi.

"Casino Venus," I said to the driver.

The car passed through the dark night roads and stopped in front of the Casino.

I walked inside down a corridor with a red carpet. Crystal chandeliers illuminated the corridor. I gave my fur to the coat check.

"Here you are, your usual number" said the man in the coat check. I took a glance at the round brass check he gave me. Fifty-one. I put it in my purse.

The revolving door that led to the interior of the Casino Venus glided slowly and opened. I went inside. The glass closed behind me. Now I was in a box made of glass. The glass in front of me opened, I came out. I was in the Casino Venus.

I took a look around. The half dim light in the interior of the Casino and the light music that attracted people to the machines filled the air. Purple, yellow, green lights blinked at me, as if they were quietly saying, "Come."

In the middle of the salon was a machine I had never seen before. It was a huge thing. It had a unique, light music. The music would play and then stop. The machine was round, it looked like a carousel. Around it there were seats, gleaming brass ashtrays, numbers, and various colored keys. In the middle a roulette wheel was turning, with the ball bouncing from here to there.

The metallic voice of a woman speaking now and then came to my ear.

"No more bets now."

It was a strange noise, coming from the depths. I asked the worker next to me, "What is this?"

"It's a new machine. It just came today. It's an automatic roulette machine. It doesn't have a living croupier. That voice you hear runs the game. You sit here, press the buttons, and pick the numbers you want. That's how it's played."

"Interesting . . ." I murmured. "This voice talking is very unusual. . . ."

"It's a tape. It gives you information throughout the game."

This shiny, unusual roulette machine without people captured my interest.

I quietly sat down on one of the leather chairs.

There was no one but me at the automatic roulette machine. I investigated the colored buttons on both sides with interest. There was a little screen in front of me. When I put my hand on a transparent little ball the screen lit up, and roulette numbers and colors appeared.

I pressed on red thirteen.

The woman's voice came from the tape,

"No more bets now," she said.

The roulette wheel in the middle began to turn. The little ball bounced off the corners and came to rest on a number.

"Thirty-three. You lost," said the metallic voice.

I lit a cigarette. Playing with the transparent ball in front of me, I was waiting for the screen to show the numbers again.

My glass of champagne and cigarettes came. I took a sip of champagne. Just as I was about to pick a number, I realized that the woman's voice was speaking.

"If you give me information about the things you've lived through, I can be of assistance to you," she said.

I was astonished.

The voice repeated what it had said.

"If you give me information about the things you've lived through, I can be of assistance to you," she said.

In bewilderment I sat there rubbing my hand on the transparent opal colored ball in front of me. The screen would come and go.

"If you're not careful, you'll break the machine," said the voice.

I took my hand off the ball.

"Excuse me; I was just taken by surprise. I didn't know what to do," I said slowly.

"No harm done. I was joking. Nothing will happen to the machine," said the voice.

"Nothing, really?"

"Nothing at all."

What kind of machine is this?"

"Taito. A Japanese machine. Made in 1991.

"Really,"

"You didn't answer my question," said the voice. "If you give me information about what you've lived through, I can be of assistance to you."

"What do you know about me?"

"Just about everything."

I was completely bewildered.

"Then you know what I've lived through. Why do you want information about it from me?" I asked.

The metallic voice laughed a little.

"It's important how you tell what happened. How you understood these experiences, how you analyzed them," it said.

"Oh, that's it," I said. I took a sip from my champagne.

In the glass enclosure in front of me the roulette wheel was spinning around, and since I wasn't playing, the ball was being thrown haphazardly from place to place.

The metallic voice repeated its question.

"If you give me information about the things you've lived through, I can be of assistance to you."

I was thinking. How could I tell it everything?

"Listen," I said. "I have an African violet I like very much. Its flowers are purple. This flower of mine stands in front of the window. It's very valuable to me, you understand. I love it. It's cheerful, happy, and full of flowers on top. Along with its leaves that are turning yellow, it has fresh new bright green leaves—a violet that is made up of several roots. For a year and a half I've been in love with it. Now a disease has struck it, a white mold like cotton, sticky bugs, a disease. This didn't bother it too much, but every morning I plucked off its dried and buggy leaves and sprayed poison all around it," I said. "I gave a shock to its roots, I confused it. I felt sorry for it, but I upset it."

"I understand," said the voice. "You wanted to get rid of those white sticky bugs to bring it back to health."

"Yes," I said. "It would have grown in a more healthy way. It would have been more comfortable. I must have upset its roots, confused all of its thoughts. My flower isn't like itself at all any more, not at all. It's faded. It's completely different. I don't know what to do."

"I understand. Now I understand everything much better," said the voice from the tape. "You shocked its roots, you upset it. You made it unhappy with you. You broke its heart. Maybe it wasn't expecting behavior like that from you."

"Yes," I said. "Everything is just as you said."

"He doesn't telephone, any more, does he?"

"Not for a while."

I drank down my champagne.

"I go and look at it every morning," I said. "I'm so worried. I'm upset and afraid."

"Are you afraid you killed it?"

"It, it's love . . . I don't know, I'm so confused . . . ," I said. I lit a cigarette.

"Wait a minute, give it a little time," said the voice from the tape.

"You think so?"

"Yes."

I put out my cigarette in the brass ashtray.

"See you tomorrow night. I'm going now," I said.

"I'll wait for you tomorrow night," said the voice.

Five minutes later I had gone outside the glass enclosed area of the Casino Venus, hopped into a cab, and arrived home.

I opened the door with my key. I threw my fur on a chair. I lit the light in the salon.

The violet was in its place. In the salon light its leaves seemed to gleam for a minute. I went quietly over to it. It was silent. Its leaves looked dull again. There was nothing left of that old lively happy feeling. It was silent. I looked at it for a while.

"Don't be crazy. Time's going by. You know I love you very much," I said. "Stop being so quiet all the time."

It just sat there.

I turned out the light and went into the bedroom. I glanced at the answering machine. There were two messages.

I moved the tape to the start and listened a few times.

I wondered if he was leaving these silent messages. . . . I didn't know.

I looked at the telephone in pain.

There was a message from him every night on the phone. He always called me from the places he went, from Diyarbakir, from Kemer, from Izmir, from Istanbul, from Gaziantep.

He knew that I'd worry, that I'd be unhappy, that I'd be happy; he knew everything about me.

The telephone was silent.

I went into the salon again. I went over to it in the darkness. I could hardly make out its leaves.

"Why are you doing this? Or didn't you ever love me at all?" I asked. "Two people can fight; people who love one another can scream and yell at one another. Then everything works out. Why are you dragging on with this? Maybe you don't love me anymore."

Everywhere was quiet.

I went back to my room and lay down on the bed. The love between two people is a very delicate crystal rod. I knew this. So he's very sensitive. Maybe he has some kind of strange pride too.

Or did he never love me?

I slipped into a lonely and anxious sleep.

≫●

Evening had fallen anew on Bartin. The shops had pulled down their shutters; curtains were drawn in the houses. The quiet streets soon become even quieter.

I came running to the door of the Taşhan. Mebrure was wrapped in her trench coat, waiting at the base of the wall. I saw that she was exhausted, with deep hollows under her eyes.

"I'm here again," she said.

"Well, were you able to get inside?"

"No. A little while ago I pushed on the door for nothing. It didn't even budge," she said. Her voice sounded hopeless.

The illusionary women were slowly coming from the various streets of Bartin to the Taşhan, hitting the door, and going inside.

A young man appeared in the darkness. He was holding a flower wrapped in cellophane. He looked at the address card in his hand and walked straight towards the Taşhan. He must be an assistant from a florist's shop. . . .

"This is the Taşhan, isn't it?" he asked me.

"Yes. Did they order from in there? Who are you taking this flower to?"

"This, it's an African violet," said the florist's assistant. "Its table has been reserved, the address is here, and I'm bringing it in."

"An African violet?"

"Yes."

I looked closely at the flower wrapped in the cellophane. I became very excited. This was the exact copy of my African violet.

"They couldn't look this much alike!" I exclaimed. "This flower is my flower!"

"I have no idea," said the florist's assistant. "This flower came from Ankara. Its table in the Taşhan is ready."

He pushed the door and went inside.

The door closed behind him.

Mebrure was asking, "What happened, what's this flower?"

"I can't believe what I just saw," I said. "This one is mine. It came from Ankara and went into the Taşhan."

"What are you saying?"

"I swear it's true."

The assistant came out. As he went off in the night whistling I collared him.

"Where did you leave the flower?"

"In the back, on the table that was reserved for it."

"Is anyone sitting at the table?"

"Not yet. The table's empty."

I sent the assistant off into the night and went over to Mebrure.

"I'm going inside. You wait for me here," I said.

I pushed on the door of the Taşhan. The door opened easily. I slipped into the dream-colored half-lit world inside.

The man was sitting in his usual place.

"Hello. I'll be right back," I said to him. I was looking at the tables in the back, trying to pick out the African violet. Suddenly I saw it. It was sitting right in the middle of one of the tables in the very back. I pulled out the chair at the table and sat down. With trembling hands I opened the cellophane on the flower in front of me and untied the ribbon.

It was a different African violet, this one! The flowers were white.

"Forgive me. I thought you were someone else," I stuttered.

"Unbelievable resemblance. I couldn't quite see the color of the flower in the cellophane."

"Please, do sit down," said the African violet. "Now we've met. What'll you drink?"

"Did you come from Ankara?"

"Yes, I came from Ankara."

"Why did you come to the Taşhan?"

"To think of someone here, to live them again," said the flower. "Would you like a cigarette?"

"Thank you," I said, and took the cigarette he held out. He lit my cigarette with an elegant gesture.

"So you came here to think about a woman?" I asked.

"Yes," said the African violet. "I came to the Taşhan to think about a woman, to live her again."

"Did you love her?"

"Yes, very much," he said in a slow voice.

"Did she love you too?"

"Yes, she loved me very much."

We were quiet for a bit.

"I came to Bartin, to the Taşhan, to think of her and live her again all night long, but suddenly I ran into you," said the African violet. He was looking into my eyes, and ordered wine.

"She'll come in a little while, your lady," I said. The sun has set.

The violet laughed.

"But I'm not thinking of her right now!" he said. "You're here with me. I want to get to know you. Let's talk, let's get to know one another. Where did you come from?"

"I came from Ankara, too."

He lifted up his glass, and looked into my eyes.

"To happiness," he said.

I drank a little wine.

"Excuse me please, now. I'm pleased to have met you," I said.

"Where are you going? You just sat down here with me," said the African violet. "I ordered fruit."

"Thanks anyway."

"Don't run away. Stay. Sit down," it said.

"I'm not running away. There's a friend over at the next table. . . ."

"Forget about him," said the violet.

"Your friend will be here soon. . . ."

The violet laughed again.

"She won't come, I'm not thinking of her right now! You're with me," he said.

The waiter brought fruit in a boat-shaped dish.

"See you again," I said as I got up from the table, and slipping among the illusionary women who were coming inside, I got myself out of there.

Mebrure was right at the door. When she saw me she became excited.

"What up? What's happened?" she asked anxiously.

"Wait, I'll tell you," I said.

Next to Mebrure, with her back to the wall, stood a young girl, a dark beauty. Her curly black eyelashes shadowed her rosy cheeks; her eyes, shaped like grapes, were staring anxiously.

She had on a white jacket and a black bustier that covered her small breasts. Her curly dark hair spread down on her shoulders. On her thin wrists she had golden chains with blue evil-eye beads. She was very alarmed. Her thin feet with repainted nails were visible between the straps of the sandals on her feet.

Mebrure said, "My friend's name is Melis. She couldn't get in anyway, either. She's being trying and trying. The door didn't even open a crack.

"Melis didn't know what to do. She pushed at the door again. The door of the Taşhan didn't even move."

"Is your guy inside?" I asked.

"Inside. He just came. That's what I heard," said Melis.

"Why aren't you going inside? Go on in to him. . . ."

"I can't open the door."

"Why, I wonder?"

"I don't know. He's a real womanizer. He must have found someone else. In a flash, just like that. . . . I can't believe it. But, see, I just push and push on the door and it doesn't open," she said.

"What's he like?"

"Well-off. Middle-aged. Considered good-looking. Dresses well."

"An African violet?"

Melis turned her black eyes to me in astonishment.

"Yes, an African violet," she said.

By my side, Mebrure muttered: "He's a male, right; they're all the same, these guys. Look, whatever he's up to, the girl can't get inside."

"What's his name?" I asked.

"Faruk Bey," said Melis.

"Did you just meet Faruk Bey, Melis?"

"Well, you couldn't say 'just met.' It's been a few months. We had some really good times together, if you know what I mean, his hand in mine, his knee on mine. . . ."

"I understand."

"He took a house for me, with a view of a lake. You can see the lake from the kitchen. We got some things. The chairs are black, the carpets salmon colored. I planted the balconies all with flowers. We made just a little nest for ourselves," she said.

"Is he married?"

"Married."

"There was a mistake a little while ago," I said.

Melis wasn't listening to me; she was just talking to herself.

"I wonder if he's thinking about his wife. The woman called him again. Why can't I get inside, I absolutely cannot understand."

"There was a mistake. I thought Faruk Bey was someone else. By mistake I went over to him and sat at his table. Maybe I got his attention at that moment, and his mind was distracted. That's when you couldn't get in," I said.

Melis was looking at me with attention now.

"You mean you saw him. . . ."

"Yes, I saw him. An African violet with white flowers. He drank a little wine. He came to the Taşhan to think of you and live for you. That's what he told me. If you try now, you can go inside," I said.

Melis pushed at the door of the Taşhan. The door opened easily and, after the girl went inside, closed noisily.

Mebrure said, "What's going on, I can't understand! Didn't you have a flower? That's what you said. It reserved a table inside, came here from Ankara. . . . What happened, did you see it?"

"It wasn't the right one. It was a different one. When I sat next to it, I realized," I said. "I thought it looked like mine. The light was dim in there."

"They're all the same, all of them," said Mebrure. Her eyes stared into the darkness.

≫₀

As I was opening the door with my key, I heard the phone ringing inside. I quickly opened the door and made it to the phone.

"Hello," I said.

"Hello," said a smoky woman's voice from the other end. "I was afraid I wouldn't find you at home."

"I just came in the door," I said. "Who am I speaking to?"

"I'm Adviye," said the woman on the other end of the receiver. "Please forgive me. I'm a little excited, I forgot to introduce myself. I'm Adviye."

I was very excited.

"Gül Abla's friend Adviye, right?"

"Yes. I have to see you as soon as possible. I have certain things to tell you. Do you have time?" Adviye asked.

"We can meet whenever you'd like," I said.

"Is right now possible?"

"Yes, it's possible." I looked at my watch. It was just evening. "Where should we meet?"

Adviye paused for a moment.

"We could meet in the Serender Patisserie in Emek," she said. "You know the place, don't you? Fourth Avenue in Emek. It's nice at this time. We can have tea together and talk."

"Fine," I said. "I'll be there in ten minutes."

I put down the phone.

A thousand thoughts were passing through my brain. Adviye had called me. She clearly had things to say. I was very curious. I wondered where Celal was. Ten minutes later I was in the Serender Patisserie.

The pastry shop was crowded. At most of the tables there were ladies sitting and chatting.

I saw Adviye right away. She was sitting at the farthest table in the back. When she saw me she stood up.

"How are you?" I said as I shook her hand. I sat in the chair across from her.

She was as I had seen her, Adviye. She was very beautiful; her hair was gathered on her neck in a bun. She had leather earrings in her small ears. She had on a suit the color of dried rose petals.

"What should we have?"

"Let's have coffee."

"Fine."

After Adviye told the waiter to bring the coffee, she leaned over towards me. There was an unusual gleam in her eyes; her voice was full of an excitement she could not hide.

"Something very strange happened," she said. "Maybe something that only you could understand. Something very hard to believe. . . ."

The waiter brought our coffees.

"I don't know where to begin, where to start explaining what happened," said Adviye.

"I'm listening to you. I'm concerned."

"Last night . . . last night I was alone in the house. I was getting ready to go to bed. Just then something very strange, something unbelievable happened. The doorbell rang. I went and opened it. I don't know if you'll believe what I'm going to tell you. Because the things I'm going to tell you aren't things that are real," she said.

"Just relax and tell me," I responded.

Adviye took a sip from her coffee.

"When the door opened I thought for a second that I would just collapse on the spot. My heart stopped from amazement and excitement. Celal was at the door. You remember Celal, don't you?"

"Of course. That young man who committed suicide," I said.

"Yes," Adviye continued. "Celal was standing in front of me. My throat was dry, my eyes were swollen in astonishment. I couldn't make a sound. It was like in a dream . . . Celal was standing right there, in front of the door. He was more excited than I was. He didn't know what to say. Finally he was able to say 'Adviye.' He looked me over from top to toe, as though he were carving all the details of my hair, my face, and my eyes one by one into his brain. He seemed to thirst for me. He was looking like he would just swallow me up. He was very young. Just like when I last saw him thirty years ago. Maybe . . . maybe he had on the same silk shirt. That's what I thought. He was very handsome. Anyway, in the thirty years that had passed, his image had faded a little in my mind. Like a sepia photograph. Seeing him suddenly in front of me like that I realized how very handsome he was. Youth . . . what I had lived and left behind, and what he still had. Youth. I took him inside. He came in very hesitantly. Neither of us really knew what to say, how we could talk. I didn't ask him how and from where he had come. I didn't even think of it. He was there, all alive, right in front of me. I was so excited. He sat down on the corner of the couch. He couldn't take his eyes off me.

"'After all these years . . . ,' he said. He couldn't even speak.

"'You're the same Adviye,' he said. 'Beautiful Adviye. Adviye with the hair that smells of jasmine.'

"I laughed. 'The years have changed me a lot, Celal. Youth flies away. It's very beautiful. I didn't know that then. In later years my soul changed, too. I experienced many things. I'm a middle aged woman now. That Adviye you remember stayed somewhere in the past,' I said.

"'No, you're the same Adviye,' said Celal. You haven't changed at all. The Adviye of my dreams. . . .'

"I wanted so much at that moment with him to be twenty five years old," said Adviye. She was both talking and looking at me. She went on.

"We sat across from one another. We didn't talk very much. We just looked at one another. Just that . . . he was so young, so handsome, so nice. It was like that intervening thirty years, the thirty years that I had lived and he hadn't, suddenly evaporated and vanished into the air of the salon. In that thirty years were my pains, my joys, my sleepless nights, my despair, everything was there. I didn't ask him at all how he came to my house. It was really Celal, alive. I realized this the second I laid eyes on him.

"What strange things I'm telling you, aren't they? You'll think I'm imagining things. But it's not imagination, it was real."

≋•

Adviye seemed to suddenly grow tired as she was telling about the strange magic spell of the night before. She leaned backed.

"What do you think about this?" she asked.

"It's an incredible thing, unbelievably beautiful. I believe you," I said.

"Then," said Adviye, "he got up and slowly walked around the living room. He looked at the pictures of my husband and my children. I was following his face.

"I noticed that a hurt look crossed his eyes. He didn't ask anything. He sat down on a corner of the couch again. He was looking at me.

"'I came for you,' he said. 'To see you. . . .'

"I quietly took his hands. I had to help him. He was so young! He hadn't lived through all the years I had. When I touched his hands, electricity I can't explain went through my body. . . ."

Adviye was leaning towards me now. She was living last night all over again, I realized.

"At that moment I wanted him like crazy. Like I'd never wanted anyone up till then. It was an incredible feeling. It was like I had run and run and outstripped those thirty years and caught up with him. I was out of breath. I saw the same gleam in his eyes. We couldn't let one another go," she said.

"The things you're saying are extraordinary things . . . ," I murmured.

"I can't forget those moments I lived last night. No one, absolutely no one could understand it," said Adviye.

Her eyes dimmed for a moment.

"I woke up early. I was full of feelings I can't explain. He was sleeping next to me. His arm was around my neck. His sleep was deep and quiet, like a child's. I got up slowly, without waking him up, and brewed some tea. I went to the bathroom and looked in the mirror for a long time. There were lines on my face. Lines left by the years. I combed my hair and tied it up. I wondered if he found me old. In any event my body, my legs, and my arms, my face, my spirit, all bore the marks of the years. I was full of thoughts. When he held me in his arms at night what had he been thinking? He kept whispering my name, 'Adviye, Adviye. . . .'"

"Celal is crazy in love with you," I said.

"And me!" said Adviye. "I had no idea that I wanted him so much. . . ."

She lit a cigarette and looked at me.

"He left. He said he was going to see a friend. He'll come again this evening," she said.

⤳•

"To the Casino Venus," I said to the driver. I put up the collar of my fur and leaned back. In ten minutes, I had passed the revolving glass door and sat down at my seat in front of the Taito automatic roulette machine. My glass of champagne had arrived. I lit a cigarette.

"Hi, what's up?" said the metallic woman's voice from the tape.

"Hello," I said. "Nothing new."

"Is your African violet still the same?"

"The same."

"Silent."

"Silent."

"Telephone?"

"Doesn't call or anything," I said.

"That means you really got to him," said the metallic voice.

"Is that the way love ends?" I asked. All these things were starting to get to me. "I told him all my feelings. What else could I do? Maybe he never loved me. . . ."

"You've started to get annoyed with him. Don't do that," said the voice.

"Yes, I'm annoyed," I said.

I polished off the champagne. I got up from my seat.

"Are you leaving? You didn't play at all. . . ."

"I don't want to play tonight. I'm not in the mood. I'll come again tomorrow."

"I'll wait for you tomorrow," said the voice coming from the tape. "Now, don't go home and do something. . . ."

"I won't, don't worry," I said.

I went into the living room and turned on the light. The African violet was in its usual place.

Going into the bedroom, I took a look at the answering machine. There was a message. I got excited. I wonder if this message was from him. I pushed the button.

"This is Irfan," said the voice on the answering machine. "Celal is with me. We'll be at the lot again this evening. I thought I'd let you know."

I went back to the living room, to the African violet.

"You're thirsty, let me give you some water."

It didn't say anything. I gave it a glass of water.

⁂

I'm walking around in Bartin. A night wind is making my hair fly around. I look carefully at the dark and silent streets. At the streets where the illusionary women would appear in a little bit and slowly make their way towards the Taşhan. . . . My eye searched for Mebrure. I had forgotten, I hadn't asked her which street she lived in. I walked on and on until I came to the door of the Taşhan. I looked, and Mebrure was there. She was wrapped up in her trench coat, standing at the corner of the wall.

"I couldn't open the door again. I couldn't go inside . . . it's a pain to stay outside the door. Every night I say, 'Let's not do this anymore,' but some strange thing pulls me here," she said.

"Look, look over there," I whispered. Mahmut's new lover Meral the Nurse had appeared at the corner of the road. She had had her hair done, her makeup was gleaming. She didn't even look in our direction. With her high heeled shoes clicking on the paving stones, she came to the Taşhan. She opened the door with a tap and went inside.

"It makes me crazy to see this," said Mebrure.

She was crying. Her shoulders were shaking, tears were flowing from her eyes.

"It's so strange," she said. It's like I'm coming here to see this. This woman going inside, to see her going in to be with Mahmut . . . So strange. . . ."

"Don't cry. Don't upset yourself. It's not worth it," I said.

"Could you do the same things for yourself?" she asked.

I didn't say anything.

≫₀

I ran up Gül Abla's stairs. When I went in the apartment, the lights were lit, as always. Gül Abla's door was open a crack. I tapped on the brass knocker and went inside. Brushing past the furs on the coat rack I went inside to the room with the couch.

"What's your hurry? Sit for a minute, take a breath. What happened, is something going on?" Gül Abla asked.

I had sat in the dried-cherry colored velvet chair with the carved wooden arms. Gül Abla was across from me.

"You're coming from the Casino Venus, aren't you?" she asked.

"Yes," I said. "I'm coming from the Casino Venus."

"Did you lose money, what happened?"

"I lost a little, but no problem," I said.

"Did you play on your male machine again?"

"No, this time I was on a very different machine. A pinball machine."

"What's that?" asked Gül Abla with interest.

"It's a fast machine," I said. "One of the Japanese Sigma machines. When you're playing it you have to be careful, as though you were driving a car."

"Allah, Allah, what kind of machine is that . . . ," said Gül Abla.

"Balls come," I said. "Two balls, three balls . . . if you're lucky four balls come at once. You push the buttons and open the balls. You can open a ball that's worth ten million, or one that's worth nothing. Besides, the balls don't come very often. When they come, they begin to spin around. The high numbers usually come from the middle and last balls. But you can't be sure of this, either. I missed a fifty million ball, I pressed the one next to it, it was a fifty," I said.

"These machines are fixed. And you're crazy about them. Look, you're worn out again," said Gül Abla. "Wait, let me make you a coffee."

"So strange," I said. "I can never get a high number ball. I always press the one next to it. It couldn't be just a coincidence."

Gül Abla called out from the kitchen.

"Those machines are all regulated. You think they're ever going to give you a high number? . . . I keep telling you, you don't listen. . . ."

Gül Abla brought in the coffee and sat across from me.

I took a sip of my coffee. My eyes fixed on the African violets in all different colors on the round table between us. I looked at them for a bit. I asked Gül Abla something which came to mind for the first time.

"Gül Abla. I'm going to ask you something."

"Ask, dear."

"These African violets . . . You love them, you take such good care of them . . . If one of them loses a leaf you get all upset."

"Yes," said Gül Abla. "I'm very devoted to these African violets"

"They are the men in your life, aren't they, Gül Abla?" Maybe the men in your past. You show particular interest in that one with the pink flower. Is that an old lover?"

Gül Abla had put on her glasses that made her eyes seem larger than they were and was looking steadily at me.

"What things you think of! Sometime I'm just astonished when I think about it," she said.

"These African violets are the men in your life. I'm sure of that, Gül Abla," I said.

She didn't say anything for a minute.

"I never thought of any such thing. How could African violets that I brought from the street be the men in my life?"

She wasn't going to tell me anything, I realized.

"That one," I said. "The old violet that doesn't bloom anymore. . . . That must be your husband, who put you through so much . . . look, you put it in the back. That little light blue one is a young lover, if you ask me. . . ."

Gül Abla began to laugh.

"What else!" she said. "That's my first fiancée, Şakir Bey, that's Kenan, who was after me for quite a while but I didn't realize it. You're amazing! What things you think of! Sometimes you astonish me. These are African violets I've had for years. That ball machine you told me about must have really affected you."

I looked into her eyes.

I realized that she wasn't telling me the truth. There were parts of her life she was hiding from me.

My eyes fixed on the African violets on the table again. The one with the pale pink flowers . . . It was so beautiful . . . It was the one that Gül Abla liked the best.

"Your eyes are fixed on the violets, and you're lost in thought . . . ," said Gül Abla.

I was thinking.

"Your fiancée who died, Şakir Bey, is that violet, isn't he, Gül Abla? The one with the different leaves, like a big twisted moustache. . . ."

Gül Abla was laughing.

"That's a double-leaf violet," she said.

"And that one, the one closest to you, with the pink flowers? That must be a lover, well-liked and cared-for. . . ."

"What things you're saying today!" said Gül Abla. "If I didn't know you don't drink, I'd say you'd been drinking. These are violets, flower plants."

From the evasive, watchful look I caught from under her glasses I knew that she wasn't telling me the truth.

When I came home it was late again. Throwing my fur on the armchair I took off my gloves. I turned on the lights in the living room and kitchen.

I looked at the African violet. It sat quietly in its place there.

"What's up, how are you?" I said to it. It didn't make any reply.

"I can't understand this silence of yours. I wonder if you're trying to upset me. But you were never like that!"

The living room was quiet.

I went into my bedroom. There was a message on my answering machine. The red light was blinking.

"I'll be waiting for you tonight when the moon sets in the Taşhan in Bartın. You remember me, don't you? We spoke together one night. I'm the African violet Faruk. I reserved our table, I'm eagerly waiting for you."

≫₀

When I arrived at the door of the Taşhan the moon was about to set. Bartın was buried in its night silence again. The illusionary women were slowly coming out of the side streets, coming to the Taşhan, pushing the door open and going inside.

Mebrure was next to the door. She was happy to see me. "I was waiting for you, where've you been?" she asked. "Listen to me, Mebrure," I said. "Go straight home. Fix yourself up. Put on something nice. Something attractive, interesting. Put on perfume, and makeup.

"Why," said Mebrure. "I can't even get inside!"

"You'll get inside tonight. Go right now and get ready, and when you come back, you'll be able to go inside."

"How will that happen? Or is Mahmut going to start to think of me again?"

"Don't lose time. Go ahead, do what I said. I'm going inside," I said.

I pushed open the door and went into the twilight world of the Taşhan.

My man was sitting at his table. I waved my hand at him. "I'll come by," I said.

In a table at the back Mahmut was sitting with his lover Meral the Nurse. They were gazing at one another. They were talking in low voices.

The African violet Faruk Bey was sitting at a big table in the middle of the court of the Taşhan. The table was spread with all kinds of hor d'oeuvres. He saw that I had come.

"Please sit down, welcome," he said.

I pulled out a chair and sat down across from him.

"Thank you very much for accepting my invitation and coming," said Faruk Bey. "I've been thinking just of you since the moment I saw you. You ran away and disappeared that day. You didn't even have a piece of fruit. What'll you drink?"

"We'll have something to drink in a bit. I have things to tell you," I said.

"Of course, of course . . . go ahead, I'm listening to you. Waiter, bring the hot things a little later."

"Faruk Bey, I have a request to make of you. It's something important."

The African violet Faruk Bey was looking into my eyes in astonishment.

"Whatever you want," he said.

"No, really."

"Faruk Bey, I'm going to ask you to think of a woman named Mebrure Hanım this evening."

The African violet Faruk Bey was astonished.

"Tonight, you want me to think of a woman named Mebrure Hanım? How can that be, when I have you in front of me? I'm only thinking of you. I don't know any woman named Mebrure, so how could I think of such a person?"

"I'll explain. I'll explain everything. Mebrure is a nice lady. Right now she's a little down because of what she's been through. I'll describe her very carefully to you. She has light brown hair, big hazel eyes, a sad face, thin body. . . ."

"Who is this Mebrure? Where did she come from? I don't understand," said Faruk Bey.

"Mebrure is the former lover of one of the men here. I don't know how many nights she's been waiting all depressed at the door of the Taşhan. There's no way she can get inside. . . ."

The African violet Faruk Bey asked with curiosity, "Why can't she get inside?"

"Because the man she loves doesn't think about her any more. He has another lover. He's in the Taşhan right now. He's sitting tête-à-tête with his new lover at one of the tables. If you think of Mebrure, she'll be able to succeed in getting into the Taşhan."

"You're really saying some unusual things," said Faruk Bey.

"You'll help her, won't you? She's an illusionary woman. When you imagine her, she can come into the Taşhan.

"How can I imagine a woman I've never seen or met?" asked Faruk Bey.

"I'll tell you about her. I'll describe her to you very well. Then if you start to think about her, she'll be able to come inside a little later."

"Okay tell me about Mebrure. What kind of woman is she?" he said.

"You've started to think about her!"

"Yes, I got curious. A young woman suffering the pain of love. Very well, what's Mebrure planning to come here and do?" asked Faruk Bey.

"She obviously wants to see the man she loves."

"You said that her lover was here?"

He looked carefully around.

"I'll point him out to you later," I said.

Faruk Bey thought for a moment.

"Mebrure will come in the way I think of her, right?"

I hadn't thought of that.

"Yes," I said. "The way you imagine her is the way she'll come in."

"In that case," said Faruk Bey. "I'm going to imagine her as very beautiful, very unusual."

"In what way?"

"The Mebrure that I imagine is not going to be the old, familiar Mebrure from her lover's past."

I was surprised. "But it will be Mebrure, won't it?"

"Of course it will be Mebrure. But as I imagine her."

"I get you," I said.

"Look," said the African violet Faruk Bey. The door of the Taşhan opened all the way. Mebrure was standing at the door. For an instant I couldn't believe my eyes. There was a stir in the Taşhan, as everyone started to look at this new woman who was coming inside.

Mahmut got up from his seat.

≫●

I was sitting with Irfan on the wall in the empty lot. The night frost had come. I glanced at Adviye's windows. The lights were on.

"When do you think Celal's going to come?" asked Irfan.

"Who knows . . . ," I said. "Within a few hours."

"There are some things eating at my brain," said Irfan. He lit a cigarette.

"Like what?"

"Celal's got used to living. He's back with the woman he loves, he's learned about slot machines, and in other words, he's right back in the middle of life. I'm afraid that he's not going to want to go back."

"He's living life as he never lived it, as he couldn't live it," I said. "He's living life to the full. He should never go back. . . ."

"But he's my responsibility," said Irfan. "I told you. I'll lose my job. I don't know what to do. . . ."

"Could you bear to take him away from life? Tell me the truth, could you actually imprison him again under that ice cold stone?" I asked.

Irfan's eyes were reflective.

"I couldn't do it," he said. "I see how he's swallowing up life. I don't know what I'm going to do. I'm in a difficult position."

"What would happen to you if they throw you out of your job?"

"I'll be jobless."

"Maybe we could find you a job. Paradise guard is a strange job anyway," I said. "You know, I never even heard of anything like that before. . . ."

"There always was such a thing, you just never heard of it," said Irfan. "Well anyway, why don't we just see how things develop?"

"Do you get a high salary? Why are you afraid of losing this Paradise guard job?"

"The salary's not high. It's regular guard's salary," said Irfan. "But there are side benefits. . . . There are the Paradise guard apartments, and then I can ride in hearses for free. I have the right for treatment in the Paradise guard dispensaries.

Things like that. . . . And of course the guaranteed right to go to Paradise when I die. We signed a paper."

"The things you're talking about all have to do with the next world, Irfan," I said. "Let's see, maybe we can find you a better job. In that case would you consider giving up the Paradise guard job?"

"I'll be fired anyway, the way things are going," said Irfan. "I placed the dead person I'm responsible for right into the middle of life. Gambling, love, sex . . . Celal, he's living all of them. How he's going to pull himself away from them and go back, I cannot imagine. Even thinking about these things in the middle of life has begun to seem strange to me. It's better not to think anything right now."

"You've come into life, too," I said. "I don't think you had very much to do with the world before."

"Not very much," he said. "I used to stand at the gate to guard Paradise and do my job. I was in charge of the 'Entered' book; in the evenings I would put my signature on the signature board. And really the best advantage was the guarantee to get into Paradise in the end. Did you know that personnel have priority?"

"Maybe you'll still go," I said.

"That's what I have to think now, at least . . . ," said Irfan.

"Well, good then. . . . Look, look, there was a movement in the curtain of the window next door, did you see it?"

Irfan carefully looked up.

"I saw it," he said. "It's Celal. Celal's shadow. I recognized him. He's most likely getting dressed."

⁂

Mebrure was standing in the threshold of the wide open doorway of the Taşhan. It was both Mebrure, and not Mebrure. I watched her in astonishment. She was very beautiful; she had turned into one of those women who get men with a single look, draw them over and turn them into moths fluttering around themselves. Her hair was platinum, falling in waves onto her shoulders. Her lips were full and gleaming, her eyes with their long lashes had a sultry look. She had on a perfectly straight, long tight black velvet dress that left one arm and shoulder exposed on top. It must have been French velvet. It clung to Mebrure's body like skin. Her exposed neck, round shoulder and pure white arm were as perfect as a statue's. Her milk-white flawless skin was in striking contrast to the black dress. A priceless diamond bracelet on the arm that was covered with velvet shone like a pole star in the dim light of the Taşhan.

Mebrure walked into the Taşhan with slow steps.

"Well, do you like her?" the African violet Faruk Bey asked me.

"Marvelous," I whispered. "Wonderful. Like a queen. Matchless beauty, striking outfit, fabulous bracelet. I can't believe my eyes. Your good taste has absolutely captivated me."

"I'm glad you liked it," said Faruk Bey. He ordered champagne from the waiter.

"I'm impressed by your strong imagination . . . ," I murmured.

The African violet Faruk Bey had imagined the country girl I had described to him as a queen, and succeeded in getting her into the Taşhan.

"Let's invite her to our table."

Mebrure paused at the door, looking around with her eyes into the smoky world of the Taşhan.

The waiter, standing next to me, murmured, "Who is this creature? We've never had a woman like that in this place before, from day one."

I waved my hand. Mebrure saw me. Smiling, she started to make her way over to our table.

Mahmut jumped up from his seat. Meral the Nurse was trying to make him sit down again.

With every step that Mebrure took, that universe the color of the subconscious in the Taşhan had waves go through it. As though men who had sat motionlessly in the same position at their tables for years suddenly came alive.

Faruk Bey, next to me, was smiling.

"A perfect female," he said. "I purposely didn't open the slit in her skirt too much, so she would look genteel. Her perfume is Paloma Picasso's latest creation, 'Temptations.' The bracelet on her arm is from Tiffany's, New York."

"You've thought of all the details!" I whispered in admiration.

"You wanted it, I did it," said Faruk Bey. "Details are what make women, aren't they?"

Mebrure had arrived at the table.

"Come Mebrure, sit," I said. The waiter pulled out the wooden chair with a flourish for her to sit down.

"How are you, Mebrure? You look very beautiful," I said.

"Thank you," said Mebrure.

"I'd like to introduce you to Faruk Bey, Mebrure. Mebrure . . . Faruk Bey. . . ."

Faruk Bey said, "I'm very pleased to meet you, Madame," as he took Mebrure's Hand, and then bent and gently touched his lips to it.

At that moment we heard someone shout, "Mebrure!"

The voice licked at the walls of the Taşhan that hadn't seen paint for years, echoed for a while around the tables, randomly collided with *rakı* bottles, then went up into the heavens above the court and vanished.

I turned and looked. It was Mahmut who was shouting. Mahmut, who looked like a pair of burning eyes. He was up on his feet. He took a step forward. His burning eyes were on Mebrure.

≈◦

I took a cigarette out of my silver case and raised it to my lips. I lit my cigarette with my lighter's trembling flame.

"To the Casino Venus," I said to the driver. I leaned back. The taxi dove into the moonless night. Ten minutes later I was at the Casino Venus. I left my fur at the coat room and passed through the glass door. Everything was the same in the casino, with its deep cherry wall-to-wall carpeting. As though time had stopped here. The multicolored machines were winking at people with their purple, green, and orange lights, calling us to a world where luck, greed, money, and a strange magic charm swirled around together.

I pulled out my leather armchair at the roulette table and sat in my usual place. My hand slowly began to move around the smooth, transparent ball. At the same time I was looking around.

A movement at the flat poker tables next to me caught my eye. A huge guy with a big nose and wide shoulders was glued to the screen and seriously playing poker. At the next three machines, young beautiful croupier girls were sitting, playing poker as well.

After I watched him a little, I noticed he was playing for very high stakes.

His eyes were fixed to the screen, and he paid no attention to his surroundings.

My champagne had arrived. I took a sip and asked the waiter, "What's going on here?"

"Sadık Bey the tobacco king," said the waiter. "You probably know him."

"No, I don't know him."

"He plays for very high stakes."

"And those girls at the machines next to him?"

"Sadık Bey is playing them, too. He took four machines. He's trying to get lucky." he said.

I asked in surprise, "Are the girls playing for Sadık Bey?"

"Yes, this way he plays four machines at once. He's definitely going to get lucky," said the waiter.

Once in a while Sadık Bey would look at the machines the girls were playing, then his eyes would revert to his own machine.

"You think he's going to win?"

"He's absolutely going to win," said the waiter. "One of these four machines has absolutely got to be lucky."

"So, he's playing four machines at once!"

"Yes, to get lucky."

I watched Sadık Bey for a while.

"You look good today," said the metallic woman's voice coming from the tape.

"I'm not bad," I said.

"How's your guy doing?"

"Last night when I went home I saw that he put out two new leaves for the first time in a month and half," I said.

"That's very good news," said the woman's voice from the tape. "That means he's slowly coming to himself."

"That's what I thought, too. I wasn't able to sleep for a while, I was so pleased and happy. It was like these two little leaves were a sign, a message to me. They said your lover is still alive. That's what I thought."

"You're right. Keep following up on it."

"That's what I'm doing," I said. "The tobacco king is playing four machines at once and trying to get lucky. It grabbed my interest."

"Yes," said the voice. "He's trying his luck."

"Do you think he'll manage to be lucky?"

The metallic woman's voice chuckled.

"Who can tell when and where you're going to get lucky!" it said.

"Maybe luck is in an entirely different machine in this salon."

"That means you think that luck is inside the machines," I said.

"If you're playing a machine, where else could luck be?" said the voice.

I was thinking.

Sadık Bey and the three croupier girls were trying to get lucky, pressing on the buttons of the machines and closely following the screens.

"Luck comes all of a sudden, doesn't it?" I asked.

"All of a sudden, all of a sudden," said the metallic woman's voice.

"In other words, it's hard to kind of grab it."

"Difficult. Sometimes, when you don't expect it to come, it does."

"How strange."

"Yes, that's the way it is."

A middle aged man sat across from me. For the first time, I was playing with someone else on the automatic roulette machine.

The man was playing with the translucent ball in front of him, waiting for the screen to come up.

"How are you, Hadi Bey?" asked the woman's voice coming from the tape.

"I'm a little better today," he said. He lit a cigar.

"Any news from your girlfriend?"

"Nothing yet," said the man.

"Why not call her?. . . ."

"I thought I'd wait a few more days."

"But you're unhappy."

"What can I do?" said the man. His whiskey had arrived. He took a sip or two, then a deep drag from his cigar.

"Why don't you call her?"

"If I call her it's not going to change anything. We'll just say the same things again."

"What did she say to you that night?"

"Leave your wife. Or you'll never see me again," is what she said.

The man sighed tensely.

"What are you thinking of doing, Hadi Bey?"

"How can I leave my wife? For one thing she's sick, my wife. Then we have all these things in common, our money. The shares in my company, the kids . . . It's all mixed up. If I leave my wife, I'll be nothing."

"But you love Gül."

"And very much," said Hadi Bey. "I told her everything. Many times. There's nothing between me and my wife anymore. It's just a formality. Sharing the same house. Sometimes we don't talk to one another the whole day long. . . . But Gül doesn't understand this, she doesn't want to accept it."

"You have it rough," said the voice from the tape. "You'll have to pick one of the two."

"I can't think of anything right now," said the man. "My mind is completely confused."

The woman's voice coming from the automatic roulette machine went silent. Hadi Bey was across from me, in deep thought. He had finished his whiskey, and asked for another.

At one point he raised his eyes and looked at me. I nodded politely. I went on playing with the opal ball in front of me.

You know, sometimes life is unbearable," said Hadi Bey. He was talking to me.

"Yes," I replied. "Life is really hard sometimes."

"My girlfriend is very young," he said.

"Really?"

"Yes. Twenty-four years old."

"You're very lucky."

He looked at my eyes.

"Is that what you say?" he asked.

"I think so," I said.

"I love her very much."

"If you won her over . . . If you talked to her . . . She probably wouldn't want to leave you."

"I don't know," said Hadi Bey. "I came here all depressed. I'm all uptight. We fought. She packed up her things and left the little house we shared, three days ago. The furs I got her are in the closet, forgotten on the hangers. She left in a hurry. She was shouting and crying. She loved those furs a lot. She was so happy when I got them. She forgot them in the closet . . . ," he said.

"Does your wife know about this relationship?"

"She knows, but she doesn't let on. She doesn't say anything. She doesn't take it seriously."

"Why don't you find Gül Hanım and tell her you love her. . . ."

Hadi Bey looked at me with anguished eyes.

"I told her. I told her many times. 'If you love me, why don't you leave her? Why aren't you willing to change your life? I don't believe you,' she said."

We were quiet for a while.

"I know, she was a chance for me. Youth, life, every single thing . . . ," added Hadi Bey.

I lowered my eyes to the screen in front of me. The numbers on the screen had been erased, and a woman's face was there.

"I'm Hadi's wife," said the woman. "His wife of thirty-five years."

She was a nice, well-kept lady. "For years I turned a blind eye to his running off and playing around. We started out life young together, and everything we have now we made together. 'He's a man,' I said, and put up with it. I made my marriage work. It's like this every time, he falls for someone. You know, just an ordinary little tart. She eats up Hadi's money, and then goes off. And Hadi says, 'I've lost the greatest chance, the best opportunity of my life,' and gets all depressed. . . . Then he comes back home."

The woman on the screen disappeared. I glanced at Hadi Bey. He was staring into the distance, puffing on his cigar.

The screen in front of me went blank again. The numbers scrambled, then it cleared up again. A young woman appeared on the screen. A charming, beautiful, fresh young woman. She had combed her reddish hair into old-fashioned long curls. She seemed like a very lifelike doll, with her false eyelashes, upturned nose and perfect skin. She had on a tight black blouse, and her lips were pomegranate red. Under the tulle blouse one could see her beautiful breasts.

"I forgot the furs in the closet, when I left. I slammed the door and left there in a rush," she said.

She lit a cigarette. When she spoke, her copper colored long curls waved back and forth, and this made her seem even more like a child than she was.

"What's going to happen to the furs now?" I asked.

"One of them is long and white, the other is a mink. I have no idea. I've got the key to the house. Maybe some time when he's not there, I'll go and get them."

"Would you think of going back to Hadi Bey, Gül?" I asked.

She opened her blue eyes wide and looked at me. She was soft and nice like a cat, this girl, suffused with sensuality.

"I don't want to go back to him," she said. "I can't go back into the cage he put me in. I had no rights, no say. He just loved me. That's what he said. 'I love you very much,' he said. I was like a kept woman. 'I love you.' Do you think that's enough? I think he found someone young in me, someone easy-going, he was able to pick up where he left off years ago. I made him laugh, I gave him a new world. But Hadi Bey had things to do, he had his own set-up, he had his own world. It's incredible. I can never be part of that world! There's no place for me in that world. That part of his life goes on and takes place without me."

"But he's in love with you."

"I'm not so sure of that," said the girl. "If he were in love, he'd leave his wife, wouldn't he?"

"I couldn't say."

"He bought me many presents. But they aren't enough. I won't go back to him. . . ."

The face on the screen vanished.

I looked over, and Hadi Bey was just sitting there.

"See you. Take it easy," I said to him. I pushed back my leather chair and stood up.

"Are you going?" asked Hadi Bey.

"Yes. I have to be someplace."

"See you."

Sadık Bey the tobacco king was at the poker table. The croupier girls on both sides were continuing to play the machines he had taken.

I asked the waiter, "Did he win yet?"

"He's just about to, but he hasn't quite done it yet."

"Think he'll do it by morning?"

"Maybe. . . ."

I left the Casino Venus.

≫•

Gül Abla took off her glasses and placed the page she had torn off the calendar down beside her.

"You're coming from the Casino Venus, aren't you?"

"Yes."

"You're thinking about something today. What happened?"

"I ran into two unusual men there."

"So who were they?"

"One was someone called Sadık Bey, who's very rich. He was playing a number of machines all at once trying to win.

"Or not to give anyone else a chance . . . ," said Gül Abla.

"I never thought of that," I said.

"Did he win?"

"While I was there he didn't."

"Since he didn't give anyone else a chance, he'll win in the end . . . ," said Gül Abla. "Who was the other one?"

"A person called Hadi Bey. He was all upset. . . ."

"Why?"

"His young beautiful lover left him."

"And he had a wife; a wife he couldn't leave, right?" asked Gül Abla.

"Yes. How do you know these things, Gül Abla?"

"It's the same old story," she said. "The guy falls for a young woman. He gets caught in a sexual whirlpool. Like his youth has come back. He buys her presents, sets up a house. The lover begins to push him to leave his wife. The guy can't undo the old web. In actually, the guy is part of the web, but he doesn't realize this. He doesn't want to do this. The young lover cries and shouts, slams the door and leaves. Putting the furs into the sports car he gave her. . . ."

"This one forgot the furs in the closet . . . ," I said.

"She's more of an ingénue than I thought," said Gül Abla. "The first thing they do is take the jewelry from the drawers and the furs. They leave the shoes behind."

I was completely bowled over.

"How do you know all these things?" I asked.

Gül Abla laughed.

"These are such ordinary things, they're always exactly the same. Boring. Did you hear all these over there? You must have been bored."

"I was bored, actually," I said.

"These things are far removed from your world. I don't know why you spend your time listening to these things . . . ," she said.

"The guy was sitting across from me. The two women appeared on the screen in front of me. . . ."

"See, always the same things . . . just as I said. First the wife, then the lover talked, right?"

"Yes."

"You were bored. Let me make you a coffee. These things are very far away from your magic world," said Gül Abla.

"But they're real, too. They're part of life."

"It's like that, there."

"Well, I'm not thinking about them anymore," I said. My eyes drifted over to the African violets on the table again. Gül Abla was making coffee for me in the kitchen. I heard the sound of the metal coffee canister she took down from the shelf. The coffeepot rattled when she put it on the stove. Gül Abla turned on the faucet, and the sound of water came to my ears.

I looked at the multicolored African violets sitting in front of me. I softly whispered to the strong violet with the broad curling leaves.

"Şakir Bey, Şakir Bey!"

"Hello?" said the violet.

"You're Şakir Bey, aren't you?"

"Yes," said the violet. "I'm Gül's first fiancée."

"Her husband . . . ," I whispered. "Which one is her husband?"

"That old violet standing in the back. He always looks out the window. Waiting for Gül. Just as he used to do."

"Which one?"

"Uhh, that one."

I looked where he pointed. A violet without flowers had turned its leaves sideways, as though it had turned its back on this little room.

"Şakir Bey. . . ."

"Hello?"

"Didn't she get along with her husband?"

"There was a big age difference between them. Twenty-five years. Gül was a young fresh thing, like a flower. She was very pretty. Her husband Rıza Bey was old. He drank a lot, God rest him. He was very jealous of Gül."

I was full of excitement.

"Şakir Bey, who is that African violet with the pale pink flowers?"

"That one over there?"

"Yes, that one with the pink flowers."

"Ah!" said Şakir Bey. "That's Cem."

"Cem?"

"Yes, Gül's young lover, Cem."

"Your coffee's coming right now," Gül Abla called out.

"Şakir Bey . . ." I said.

"She'll hear us, be careful!"

"Why did she leave you? Why did you break up?"

"We broke our engagement on an autumn day," said Şakir Bey. He suddenly became quiet.

Gül Abla came into the room with the coffee tray in the hand.

"There's your coffee. And the water's next to it. I took it from the earthen jar. So light up a cigarette and relax. I find you very serious today."

She went over and sat down across from me.

From the distance, somewhere in the house, that old wall clock rang out for a long time in some other time system again, letting us know once more about the passing of life.

I lit up a cigarette.

The African violets on the table were quiet and peaceful, as always.

Gül Hanim reached out and plucked off a leaf from Şakir Bey that had dried out, and threw it in the garbage can next to her.

≫•

I finished my champagne and got up from my leather chair next to the roulette table of the Casino Venus.

"Where are you going?" said Hadi Bey. "We didn't even get a chance to talk today. You didn't play either."

"I'm bored. I'm not going to play tonight. I have a friend who's old, I was thinking of going to see him," I said.

"Time's just not passing today. I feel the time lying on my heart like caked wax . . . ," said Hadi Bey.

"You might hear from Gül Hanım tomorrow."

"I don't know. Her furs are still hanging there in the closet."

"Maybe that's a good sign. . . ."

"You think so?" asked Hadi Bey.
"Well, maybe . . . ," I said.

≫∘

In the taxi, as I reclined on my way home, I thought of a number of things. I suddenly felt myself released from the stressful state I was in and lost myself in memories.

When I got home, I lit the lights in the living room. My violet was there in its place. I bent down and looked at the two new leaves it had put out. I sat in the chair next to it.

"You cannot imagine what I thought of in the taxi on the way home tonight," I said to it. "Do you remember, once in Bodrum, you came to me. I was waiting for you in the garden. You didn't know the house yet. You had called from over by the Tepecik Mosque. You were three hundred meters away from me. You were tired, you had come from a long overnight trip. I met you at the garden gate. You had admired the tropical plants in my garden, then sat for a while and relaxed in the coolness of my living room. It must have been August.

"We got in the car and drove around the Bodrum area. When we passed Torba Bay, you couldn't resist the deep blue sea visible below you, and you ran down the hill and swam a little. I sat on the grass and watched you. When we were going to Yalıkavak, we turned onto a wrong road, as we always did. We came upon a flat place I had never seen before with hundreds of fig trees. We got out of the car and went over to the fig trees. You were picking figs off the trees and giving them to me. Some of trees' figs were as sweet as honey, and some were different. We went inside the circular cistern at the side of the road and looked at the still, dark water in the bottom. You stamped your feet on the ground and made me listen to their echoes in there. You were as happy and content as a child there with me. Chickens and young fluffy chicks came over to the car. We chased them off for a while. It was so strange, we could never figure out the road to Yalıkavak. Suddenly Gündoğan appeared in front of us, with its deep blue bays and purple bougainvilleas. We looked at the sea from the hill for a bit. You were bringing the car downhill over narrow roads, over the rocks and cliffs. I was scared to death. At one point I closed my eyes.

"'We just can't get out of here. Are we inside a magic spell, or what!' you said, and laughed.

"Finally we got to Yalıkavak. It was as though a different sea emerged in front of us, different hills embraced us. You turned onto a mountain road again. There was a flat place on top of the hill. We came to a village. In the coffeehouse of Çardaklı village, we sat with the old men and drank tea. Looking down from the hill, one could see Yalıkavak and the sea in the distance.

"This place was Kamil Çobanoğlu square. The last time I went to Bodrum I went back there again. The *çardak* where we sat and the glassed-in coffeehouse above it were closed. The season was over, winter had come.

"Down the hill, I found another coffeehouse where the old people played checkers, and I went in there.

"I asked the coffeehouse owner. 'Who was Kamil Çobanoğlu?'

"'He died in a car accident at a very young age,' said the coffee man. 'He was very young. He flew over with his car. He wasn't even twenty-seven. The municipality gave his name to the square.'

"In the down-at-the-heels coffeehouse, as I sat amid the sound of checkers, I thought of Kamil Çobanoğlu. I thought I'd tell you all of this."

The violet was listening to me. I realized that. His ears were on me.

"In Bodrum we never went into the house for two days, do you remember?" I said to him. "At night we went to the Club M. I passed time on the machines, and you were playing blackjack. I watched out of the corner of my eye. Nearby there was an old gambler who was half-drunk. It was clear that he never went home, and passed time on the machine until the morning. Once in while he called out, 'Blackjack, Blackjack!' with a voice that came out of his nose. He was talking a lot. He seemed to be interested in me.

"It was morning. The Club M was closed. We went outside. The sky was getting light. A quiet Bodrum morning began. We got into the car again. You had business in Salihli, Aydın, Kula.

"'Can you make the trip?' you asked.

"'I can make it,' I said. I put on my sunglasses and got into the car.

"We were going along, passing over a number of tree-covered hills I didn't recognize on narrow roads. I hadn't slept. The fuel light on the car lit up.

"'How far can the car go with the light lit?' you asked me.

"'It goes a hundred kilometers!' I said. I made it up. You laughed.

"Much later in an open space we climbed up to, we must have been on the Salihli road; you pulled into a gas station, put the seat back, and slept for a little while. As you slept, I looked at you. You know, I miss those times we slept together in the car. While you were asleep a villager came over to the car from the gas station. She stared at you. 'He must be very tired. He's sleeping like a child,' she said.

"In Kula you sat me down in the park and went off to do what you had to do and then come back.

"It was a very unusual park. Full of trees and dark. Old men were sitting at the rough tables. A part Arab man with sky blue eyes was nice to me, ordered tea, and asked me where

I was from and where I was going. There was a dwarf sitting in the corner. The white Arab's hair was completely white. When he smiled I noticed that his bottom teeth were covered in gold and his upper teeth in silver. There was no other woman in the park. All of the old men were paying attention to me.

"The white Arab was chatting with me, and ordered another tea. You suddenly appeared at the top of the road. You came right over to me. The white Arab moved away a little when he saw you. We left the park together. The dwarf, the white Arab, the old men, they were all looking at us from behind.

"I can never forget that park in Kula, the shadows of the trees that reminded one of the deepness and shadows of the years, the old men sitting beneath them.

"After Aydın, Kula, Bozdağ, and Salihli, we passed along the shore of Lake Bafa and came back to Bodrum at midnight. Your eyes were full of sleep.

"'Come sleep a little.'

"'If I lie down I'll never get up.' You were driving the car on dark, dangerous twisting roads. In a little while we would go through that scary tunnel. I had no idea where it was, but you pulled the car into another service station. You went and washed your face. We were both sleepy. We put down the seats. You locked the car doors. You were trying to sleep and relax a little. I understood in those two days how exhausting your life was.

"Outside, the lights of the gas station reminded me of some strange amusement park. For a while I looked at a brightness that seemed like artificial moonlight. We must have been some-place near Bodrum. See, it's so strange, I don't know where it was. I should have asked you, you'd have told me. . . . Just at midnight we got to Bodrum. We went straight to Club M.

"The old gambler was at the table. It was clear that he was there losing every night. He said hello cheerfully.

"'Blackjack!' he shouted, calling out for them to come with the cards."

≫◦

I glanced at my violet. I was sure he had listened to everything I had said. I put out the living room lights. I stood at the door for a minute and told him a detail I had thought of.

"I got really worn out that day, but as I just said, I understood your life on the road a lot better. We were in Salihli. They had set up the open-air market. There was dust in the air or something; anyway, something got in my eye. Tears started to pour out of both of my eyes. My black sunglasses were covering my eyes, but you saw the tears slipping down my cheeks, and were very frightened. We went right into a pharmacy and got eye drops. I put the drops in my eyes in the car.

"In Bozdağ we drank ice cold water. That water was so good . . . I got bunches of sage and oregano there. All winter long when you came over, we'd sit together and drink that sage tea. . . . 'We'll go there again, won't we? Bozdağ was so pretty . . . That water like ice we drank in the shade there . . . We'll go there again, right?' I would ask you.

"You'd look happily at me. 'We will go,' you'd say.

"'We'll get sage again there.'

"'Okay.'"

I went into my bedroom and went to sleep.

≫◦

Gül Abla's door was ajar. I slowly slipped inside. Pushing past the furs hanging on the coat rack, I went into the room with the little couch where we always sat. Gül Abla had fallen asleep in her armchair. It was clear that she had dozed off while waiting for me. She held her green worry beads tightly in her right hand, and was breathing regularly through her mouth.

Without waking her up, I slowly sat in the velvet armchair.

"Şakir Bey," I whispered.

"Hello?" said the violet with the strong curved leaves.

"Were you asleep? I didn't wake you up, did I?"

"No, we never sleep. When the lights go off at night we close our eyes, that's all . . . ," said Şakir Bey.

"I slipped out and came over thinking that we could talk a little, gossip a little."

"Good idea. Gül fell asleep. She'll wake up in a bit. Fasting throws her off."

"I know. . . . Şakir Bey, is Gül Abla's husband Rıza Bey always quiet like this?"

"He's had too much to drink. He's plastered. But don't mind, he's really a good guy."

"Does he drink a lot?"

"He begins in the morning."

I lowered my voice way down.

"And Cem? Gül Abla's young lover Cem . . . You know, that violet with the pink flowers . . . Can I talk to him, you think?"

"Of course you can talk to him. He loves strangers," said Şakir Bey.

"When did Cem become Gül Abla's lover?"

"Long years ago."

"Were they really in love with one another?"

"Gül really fell for him."

"How old was Gül Abla at that time?"

Şakir Bey thought for a moment.

"Gül was about forty-five. Cem was twenty-five."

"Interesting," I said. "Was Gül Abla married then?"

"Of course she was married," said Şakir Bey the African violet. "Her husband was drinking all day long. He was insanely jealous about Gül. Gül was very beautiful. She met him in the dentist's waiting room, Cem. With Cem, Cem, she just immediately got taken with how attractive he was. And Cem was very handsome. Like a kid. Untouched, unspoiled . . . He surely got her attention. How their relationship began, where they first talked to one another, how they got together, I don't know. Cem will tell these things. Cem! Cem!" Şakir Bey called out.

Gül Abla suddenly opened her eyes.

"When did you get here? Were you sitting there silently all by yourself? Why didn't you wake me up?"

She had sat up and was fixing her hair clips.

"I got here a little while ago. I was sitting and resting, Gül Abla," I said. "I didn't want to wake you up."

"I thought I heard a voice," said Gül Abla. "Somebody in my sleep was calling an old name. The human memory is such a strange thing . . . Between sleep and wakefulness . . . Living and imagining . . . An old voice, it was calling another old name. . . . I just dozed off where I was sitting. . . ."

I stared at Gül Abla. I was trying to think of what she was like at forty-five. She must have been very beautiful. Somewhere in Gül Abla's albums she must have pictures of Şakir Bey and Cem. She had never mentioned the photographs, and if she had them, she hadn't shown them to me. I knew that she had torn up the photographs of her husband Rıza Bey and thrown them out.

"He put me through a lot. I don't want to remember him," she had said.

"What are you thinking about now?" asked Gül Abla. "You've gone off far away. . . ."

"I'm thinking about a machine in the Casino Venus," I said.

"Can't you find anything else to think about, my child?" said Gül. "Who thinks about a machine? Are you thinking about your 'male' machine?"

"No," I said. "There's a new machine in the Casino Venus. It's a machine with lips."

"A machine with lips?"

"Yes, lipstick, lips, with a bottle of perfume, a unique machine."

"What kind of thing is it?"

"Instead of numbers, bars, and cherries, there are pictures of bottles of perfume, lips, and lipsticks. If four lipsticks come into line at the same time the machine gives out a jackpot, you know, the big payoff. If two lip prints come together, the machine turns by itself eight times. If three lip prints come, twenty; if four lip prints come, it turns fifty times. And when it does this, lips can still come together at the same time. It's really fun. They just recently put it up in the back," I said.

"These machines are interesting," Gül Abla muttered.

"Yes. They really fascinate me. I really like this machine with lips."

"You've forgotten your male machine."

"Yes, I really have," I said. "And there were times when he used to jerk me around and wear me out. He gave the diamonds to another woman right in front of my eyes. Compared to these new machines he started to seem slow and boring to me."

"Oh, you faithless thing!" said Gül Abla, laughing. "Sit, I'll bring you some fruit compote. I made it from dried plums."

Gül Abla went to the kitchen.

"Cem!" I said, whispering. "Cem!"

"Yes!" said the African violet with the pale pink flowers.

"How did you meet Gül Abla?"

The leaves of the violet seemed to tremble for a minute. He was remembering that day, I realized.

"She was sitting in the dentist's waiting room. I'll never forget that day. It was just at evening. She had on a red tailored suit with a black fur collar. Ruby red . . . Her bright blonde hair was down around her shoulders. A pair of long, shapely legs like I'd never seen crossed one on top of the other. The seams of her stockings were perfectly straight. Our eyes met. For a second I felt a shock of electricity go through my whole body. She was an absolute female. A woman from head to toe. . . ."

Cem's voice was full of excitement.

"Then what happened?"

"She smiled at me a little. I couldn't be positive. Did she really smile at me? I smiled too. She went in to the dentist. I waited for her to come out. We left the dentist's together. They gave her a needle in the gum, so she was a little dizzy. There was a lipstick mark on her handkerchief. When she went down the steep stairs of the apartment, I took her arm and helped her. Her shoes had such high heels . . . I . . ."

"Here's the compote," said Gül Abla. "I brought a napkin too. Pull that little table over in front of you. There are also three dates in the little bowl. I break my fast with them."

⇛⁕

My eyes were fixed on Bartin Creek as it silently flowed in the darkness. I must be somewhere on the street with the hanging vines. I was wandering in the night through the completely empty streets of Bartin. Outside of all the doors, windows, drawn curtains, lowered gates, and closed wooden shutters. Looking for traces of him in Bartin. Walking along streets that he had once walked, looking as he had looked at the slowly flowing Bartin Creek while leaning on the metal railing of a bridge. I missed him. I wanted him to come suddenly around some corner and for us to embrace.

≫●

I was together with the night. Completely alone. The Taşhan with its men and illusionary ladies inside was somewhere along the side of the road.

The African violets on the round table in Gül Abla's little room with the couch would have their eyes closed at this hour.

"I'm completely alone," I murmured. "Really, I'm completely alone in this world."

"You're not alone, I'm here with you," said a voice in the darkness.

Everything was pitch black. There was no one visible.

"Am I truly not alone?" I asked.

"You know me very well," said the voice.

"Have we known one another for a long time?"

"You've known me as long as you've known yourself."

"Are we childhood friends?"

"You could say so. You could say we were childhood friends."

"But this is the first time that I'm hearing your voice. It's not a voice I recognize," I said.

"I'm talking to you for the first time, that's why," he said.

"We never spoke before?"

"We spoke, but in different ways."

I was intrigued.

"Do I really know you?" I asked.

"You know. You like me," said the voice.

"So we spoke before."

"We've been talking for years."

"Then you know my life."

"I know certain parts very well."

I walked in silence for a while.

"Would you tell me who you are?" I asked.

"You still haven't figured out who I am?" he said laughing.

"No, I haven't. I'm trying to, though."

"I'm together with you when the sun sets," he said. "Every day after the sun sets, I'm with you."

"Are we together for a long time?"

"Till morning. . . ."

"In that case, we're spending an important part of my life together," I said. "The real part of my life begins at night."

He was giggling next to me.

"I know, I know everything," he said.

"Everything?"

"Everything. . . . The casinos you go to, those colorful worlds you love, the machines that fascinate you, the evenings that you sit with him in the living room, that you make sage tea together, the times when you go out with him in the car to look at the moon, when you go to Gül Abla, when you talk to the African violets, Celal, Adviye, the Taşhan, I know all of it."

I was astonished.

"You must be very close to me," I said.

"Yes, I'm very close to you. I'm right here with you," he said.

"Who are you, tell me please!"

"You actually realize who I am, but you don't want to believe it," he said.

"I don't know, I'm thinking of something, but I'm not sure," I said. "Tell me, who are you?"

"Should I say? . . . Or do you want to leave it like this?"

"Tell me. I want to know."

"Why not leave it like this? We'll talk once in a while.

"Why are you hiding yourself? You know everything about me. Tell me, who are you?"

"I'm the Night," he said in a natural way. "Didn't you realize? The Night that wraps around you."

I was stunned.

"Look, you're startled now. I wasn't going to say anything to you. Now you'll be afraid of me. You won't talk. That's why I didn't want to tell you. . . ."

"So you're the Night . . . ," I whispered.

"Yes."

I was trying to think.

"Then you're very huge, very strong; after a certain hour you cover half the world, you have thousands of things going on inside you . . . ," I murmured.

"I keep a lot of things to myself, but I do have incredible things going on," he said.

"Night . . . so you're the endless Night. . . ."

"Yes."

"A big part of my life. The time I spend asleep."

"Yep, that's me," he said.

"You're wandering around the empty streets in Bartin with me."

"I'm going around with you because I know you like to live."

"You're very powerful," I whispered.

"I know," he said.

"All the magical things are in you. Dreams, illusions . . . Terrifying things, too . . . Murders, running away, deaths, births, couplings in love nests . . . lovers' trysts, husbands staggering home blind drunk . . . then watchmen with shrill whistles, duty police stations, colorful music halls, dim night clubs where naked girls do dirty dancing on tabletops, the endless half-finished rambling stories of drunks, wedding nights, celebrations, lovers' walks in the moonlight . . . They're all within

THE EMPEROR TEA GARDEN * 119

you. It's unbelievable! You're very rich and powerful. You're with me, you're here with me, we talked . . . ," I said.

"Yes," he said. "We've become friends. Are you happy?"

It was as though I were enchanted: the Night was next to me, he was talking to me. I could really feel him.

I had spoken for the first time with the Night, who had enchanted me my whole life long and had always drawn me to him in some strange way. We were walking together in the streets of Bartin.

A thousand thoughts were racing through my brain.

How powerful the Night was, and how powerful that endless magic spell.

"You know, you're very rich," I said. He was laughing.

"I don't know. Do you think so?"

"You're very rich. You keep endless things inside you. I'm just amazed when I think of it. Next to you the day is poor. Daytime always does necessary things, serious things. But night . . . Night is the part of time when everything can happen at any moment," I said.

"When you say 'night' to some people, they think of sleep," said Night.

"They don't know the Night . . . ," I said.

"The Casino Venus opens at night, for example."

"Yes, the Casino Venus opens at night. And not just that, a whole range of other secret, lit-up or half lit things open at night. The moon and the stars are yours too, aren't they?"

"The moon, the stars, the Milky Way, they're all mine," he said.

"The Taşhan comes alive at night too. The illusionary ladies come when the moon sets."

"You really like me," he said, "There are those who are afraid of me. People who are afraid to be alone in their houses, people who get sicker at night, people who are afraid of dying, of being killed . . . I don't know, there are a lot of people who are afraid of me."

"I know," I said. "But I'm not one of them."

"That's why I'm here with you, that's why I talked to you, you know . . . ," he said.

⤳•

I ran up the steps to Gül Abla's apartment. I was out of breath. I knocked with the brass door knocker. Gül Abla was there in front of me.

"What happened? You're out of breath. Were you running? Where are you coming from?" she asked.

I threw myself down in the velvet armchair with the wooden arms.

"You're so excited, what happened? Where are you coming from at this hour? Were you in the Casino Venus?" Gül Abla was asking in concern.

"Stop, let me rest a little, then I'll tell you," I said.

At the last minute I decided not to tell Gül Abla that I had been talking with the Night. She wouldn't have understood, wouldn't have believed me. Whereas I was well aware of the huge, endless dimensions of what I had lived through. I was still excited.

"The machine with the lips?" asked Gül Abla. "Was there something on the machine with the lips?"

"Yes," I said. "Four lips came together next to one another above the line. Four pink little kisses! The machine started to turn fifty times on its own. At the same time it was playing light music. During these turns, lips came together two or three times, and the machine turned seventy times altogether! Counting to itself all the time. . . ."

"It must have been incredible!" said Gül Abla. "If you only took the money and left."

"That's what I did."

"You did the right thing. Let me make us some coffee, and we can sit together and drink it."

"All right, Gül Abla."

Gül Abla went to the kitchen and turned on the light. I heard the sound of the tin can being taken down from the shelf. I bent down to the African violets sitting silently on the table.

"Şakir Bey, how are you?" I whispered.

"I'm fine. And how are you?" asked the African violet with the big curved leaves.

"I'm very excited. I spoke with the Night," I said.

Şakir Bey said, "So you spoke with the Night. That's a wonderful thing. Deep, thought-provoking . . . hard to believe. A person could talk about so many things with the Night. I'll think about this for hours," he said.

"Yes, a person could talk about this for hours, for sure."

"You could ask him everything you were interested in. Did you?" said Şakir Bey.

"The things I'm interested in?"

"Yes. He knows everything that's night, mysterious events, secrets, all of it."

"So he knows all the secrets, everything . . . ," I murmured. "Next time, I'll ask him. I was so excited, I didn't even think of it."

"Night hides everything, but knows everything as well," said Şakir Bey.

I was so impressed with the deep thoughts of the African violet Şakir Bey. He was very sensitive.

"Hello!" said the African violet with the pale pink flowers from the other side.

"Hello, Cem. We never got to finish our conversation. We got cut off at the most exciting point. Years ago, the first day you saw Gül, you went down the steep stairs of the dentist's office together. . . ."

"Yes, I can still smell the perfume she wore," said Cem. "It was a strange thing to be so close to that beauty, that femininity. 'You put yourself out to help me. Please come to my house and have a cup of coffee,' she said to me. ' . . . if you have the time.'

"Okay, I said. It was as though I were drunk. I followed behind her as though in a dream. She stopped a taxi. We got in together. She gave an address to the driver. A little while later we were in her building. I was very excited. I think she realized that. She was an experienced woman. She opened the door with the key. We went into a living room that was half lit, with the curtains closed. And it was from that moment on that my life changed!"

⋙∘

"Our coffee's ready," said Gül Abla. "You take the one with the foam. Pull the little table over in front of you, be comfortable. Then, light up a cigarette to relax, and tell me what happened. . . ."

⋙∘

I was going to meet up with the Night a little later. I walked aimlessly through the streets, waiting for the sun to set. Everything around me, living or not, was getting ready for the night. A little later the sun set, the sky grew dark. The metal shutters on the shops were being closed with a rumble, lights began to appear in the windows of the houses. The cars, busses, trucks, and vans had lit their lights.

"Hello," said a voice next to me.

I turned in excitement and looked. I couldn't see anyone. It had become really dark. Night had come.

"Hello, how are you?" I said. "We're going to go around together everywhere, aren't we?"

"Yes, we'll go look at every place you want together," he said.

I started to walk, with Night by my side.

"You know, I thought about you a lot," I said.

"Really? What about me did you think of?"

"Everything about you. You're very open-hearted. I thought of your strength. There are so many things contained in you. I could ask you questions endlessly, I could learn so many things from you. I thought about all this. All the secrets are hidden in you, all the magic, illuminated worlds are in you. . . . You're here with me right now, but at the same time you're everywhere. . . ."

"Yes, I'm everywhere. I've started. The clocks are showing me now," he said.

"You're everywhere now, in homes, hotels, police stations, all the towns, airports, coffeehouses where poor souls are hanging out, chic receptions where champagne is flowing like water, hospital rooms, between new brides and bridegrooms, dressing rooms at the opera, in concert halls, on the endless plains . . . everywhere."

"Yes," he said. "I'm in train stations, I'm in bedrooms where ladies are getting dressed while they wait for their lovers, I'm in seaside restaurants where the hor d'oeuvres are starting to fill up the tables, I'm in the insane asylums, I'm in the dressing rooms where the ballerinas are powdering their breasts and under their arms. . . ."

"How marvelous!" I murmured. "You're endless. . . ."

And so we walked along.

Night was relaxed. Night was used to the streets.

Suddenly we heard some drunk singing from the side of the road. It was strange, moving voice. It echoed in the street.

"A drunk," said Night. "And obviously depressed. . . ."

I looked towards where the song came from. On the corner of the sidewalk, there was an African violet sitting in a pot on the ground. Could the deep voice we had just heard have come from this flower?

"What's that?" asked Night.

"There's an African violet at the side of the road. Let's go look."

I went over to the violet.

A deep "oof" sound filled the whole street. The sound was coming from the African violet on the ground. I knelt down and looked at it closely. It was leaning against the wall of its pot.

"Do you have a problem? You made such a deep 'oof,'" I said.

"I have a problem," said the violet. "I'm someone who's wasted his life. Life is over."

This remark made my hair stand on end.

"Life is over?"

"Yeah, life has been over from some time, but I'm still alive. If you call this life . . . ," said the violet. I looked, and there was a half-finished bottle of vodka standing next to him.

"Do you drink a lot?"

"I drink. What am I supposed to do if I don't drink?"

The sorrow and despair in his voice touched me.

"Who are you? What's your problem?" I asked.

The African violet laughed bitterly.

"Is it important who I am? But I'll tell you. My name is Rıza. I'm an old general's son. As far as my problem, my problem is a woman called Gül."

"A woman called Gül? Your lover?"

"No, my wife. Gül's my wife."

My hair stood up. The violet I was speaking to was Gül Abla's husband Rıza Bey.

"Is she a blonde, Gül?"

"Yes, she's blonde. Don't tell me you know her?"

"I know a blonde Gül Hanım. She lives in Ayrancı. She's my friend," I said.

"Ah!" said the African violet. "You know her. She ruined my life," He reached out for the vodka bottle next to him and took a gulp.

"The Gül Hanım I know is a very sensible person. I don't understand how she could have ruined your life," I said.

The violet laughed bitterly.

"How would you know, how would you understand, are you her husband? Have you shared the same bed?" he asked.

"I'm her friend."

"Friendship is different. I gave my life to her. My life is finished. She finished me."

"You used to drink a lot, Rıza Bey. Everything happened because of that," I said.

"So she told you. . . ."

"She didn't exactly tell me, but I understood."

Without even listening to me, how can you know everything, a whole life?" asked Rıza Bey.

"You're right. I can't."

"How would you know? She didn't even see me. Her young lover Cem, her old fiancée Şakir Bey, her endless demands and moods, how would you know about these. . . ."

I was bewildered. I didn't know what to say.

"Forget about me," said Rıza Bey. "Just keep on going. Forget you even saw me. She's alone with her lover the young guy now. I drink so that I don't see anything, so that I just forget everything. They come to the house, and I'm stoned in the chair. But I see everything. Gül doesn't even look my way. They go inside, into the room. He's this young guy, she's completely head over heels for him, she doesn't see anything else in the world. The neighbors, the neighborhood, everybody's figured it out. And I'm there, in a corner of the house, with my bottle of booze by my side, The Old General's Son Rıza Bey, I just shrivel up and go to bed. My eyes are always shut tight. But my ears hear everything."

"I don't think she could possibly be that insensitive," I said.

"She's a woman," said Rıza Bey. "A woman. A woman wanting a man, seeking excitement. She did everything to me. She finished my life. I couldn't bring myself to leave that house. I couldn't escape that bizarre arrangement. I was like an invalid left on a stretcher. For years. . . . Cem didn't see either, and just passed me by. Isn't it strange? I was like some old household object for them, an old cushion, a basin, a pitcher. But I saw everything, heard everything, knew everything."

"Terrible . . . ," I said. "I'm so sorry."

"Don't be sorry. Leave me alone. Go on your way." Rıza Bey closed his eyes.

Night, next to me, said, "What happened? You've had a sudden shock. Whatever that violet tossed by the side of the road said really affected you."

"Let's get away from here," I said. I'm very upset. "That was the husband of one of my friends. He told me things I didn't know. I was astonished."

"Come," said night. "Let's go somewhere else. We'll talk."

"Stop!" we heard a voice say. "Stop, don't go!"

It was a woman's voice. It rang out at the top of the street.

Night and I stopped where we were. I was trying to get my eyes used to the darkness. There was a woman coming straight towards us.

"Don't go! Wait for me. . . . I have things to say too. You shouldn't just listen to one side . . . ," she called out to us.

When I looked closely, I saw that the person coming was Gül Abla. But not the Gül Abla that I knew. The one who was coming was a young woman. She seemed very nervous and anxious. She was walking quickly towards us, and her high heels were making sharp sounds on the sidewalk.

"Don't believe what he said!" she shouted. "He's telling everything his own way. All the things I did for him . . . He didn't mention them at all, did he? I wonder how I even put up with that life." She turned to Rıza Bey. "Do you hear me, Rıza? You don't hear me. The days and nights you left me alone . . . did you forget them? A husband in the house who's both there, and not there . . . The Old General's Son Rıza. . . . Did you ever act like a husband for even one day? Tell me, did you ever take me by the arm and go around with me?"

Rıza Bey opened his eyes and was looking at Gül Abla. "Did you even once say something sweet to me?" he whispered in a pained voice.

"Would you have been able to hear it?"

"And that young lover's girlfriend . . . Did you ever think of her? They were going to get married. You stole that young guy away from her. He couldn't see anyone else but you. That poor girl came to me, did you know that? Her name was Ayşe. You kidnapped the boy from her. She was crying. She wanted to know about you. She told me about it. I told her, too," said Rıza Bey.

Gül Abla was flabbergasted.

"Cem's old lover came to you? When? You never told me about this. This is something that happens in every man's life. A passing fancy . . . An old lover . . . I am completely astonished, you mean she came and talked to you?" she said.

"Yes, she spoke to me," said Rıza Bey. "She was totally depressed. She told me about her lover. It broke my heart to listen to her. I sat and spoke with her for a long time one afternoon. She didn't know about 'Men.' I told her about men. She told me about Cem, and I told her about you. We talked like two cast-off people thrown in a corner. It got dark in the house, the shadows grew long. She got up and left."

"All these years you never told me about that," said Gül Abla.

"How could I say anything?" said Rıza Bey. "Was I supposed to tell you about how meaningless I was in your life?"

"Be quiet! You're exaggerating everything. . . . This girl, was she pretty?"

"Blonde, blue-eyed. A beautiful slim girl. She had the freshness of youth."

"So you ripped me to pieces with some girl you didn't even know. . . ."

Rıza Bey and Gül Abla's voices were echoing in the empty street.

Night leaned over to my ear.

"The summing up of a life, a relationship, a marriage . . . ," he said.

"Yes. It's so terrible . . . I don't want to hear any more. Let's get away from here."

We left Gül Abla and Rıza Bey in the dark street and walked off in another direction.

⋙●

I was in Bartin. The humid air lapped at my face. The Taşhan was across from me. I pushed at the door and went inside.

My man was in his usual place. The African violet Faruk Bey was sitting at his table. Mebrure was next to him. The whiskey had been opened and fruit brought to the table. I looked, and saw that Mahmut was at the table as well, sitting across from Faruk Bey with his eyes fixed on Mebrure.

"Sit down, sit down. . . . Where've you been?" asked Faruk Bey when he saw me. The waiter pulled out the chair, and I sat down at the table.

Mebrure had lowered her eyes with their long lashes to the table, and was just sitting there.

Faruk Bey said, "Let me introduce you. Mahmut." Mahmut bowed in his place and shook my hand.

Faruk Bey continued on.

"Mahmut Bey is a very unique kind of friend. He claims to be Mebrure's lover. He wants her to come to his table."

"I love her so much," whispered Mahmut.

"Good, well what would Mebrure say to this?"

"Mebrure Hanım prefers not to speak."

I looked at Mebrure; she was silent.

Mahmut said, "She should come to my table. I can't figure out what she's looking for around here."

Faruk Bey said, "But I thought of her. I imagined Mebrure Hanım and she easily came into the Taşhan. And now, of course, she's going to sit at my table."

Mahmut said, "I thought about her for years. I love her, I love her a lot."

Mebrure, who had been silent until then, suddenly raised her head and looked at Mahmut.

Her eyes were full of pain and cold.

"I tried the door of the Taşhan for days on end. I could never push it open and get inside. The door wouldn't even open a crack. It was so hard, so pitiless. That door was your heart, your mind. You didn't think of me even for an instant. I was outside, in the cold and the darkness, with one hope. I suffered a lot outside the door. But you didn't even think of me then. Did you just start to think of me now? Go to your own table. There somebody waiting for you there. Go on, what are you waiting for, I'm staying at this table." she said.

Mahmut's face became like chalk. He suddenly put his hand in the inside pocket of his jacket. He pulled out a revolver. The Taşhan was filled with the scream of the woman sitting at the next table. Mahmut pointed the barrel of the revolver at Mebrure.

Everything was happening so quickly. I was so surprised I didn't know what to do.

"So that's the way it is," said Mahmut.

The woman at the next table continued to scream. Everything became confused in the Taşhan. The gun erupted with a deafening roar. A thick smell of sulfur spread around. Everybody had stood up from their tables. Women's screams were echoing from the yellowed old walls of the Taşhan.

Mebrure sat where she was.

Mahmut was distraught. They grabbed him and took the gun from his hand. I looked at Mebrure. She looked a little yellow. She fixed her hair with her hand. Someone took my arm.

I realized that Night was by my side.

"There are terrible things going on, but Mebrure didn't die," I said.

"He can't kill her. He can't do anything. She's an illusionary woman, isn't she?" he said.

"Right. She's an illusionary woman, Mebrure. Maybe it's impossible . . . ," I said.

"Yes," said Night.

Everything was in confusion.

"Come on," said Night. Let's get out of here. Nothing happened. We'll come back again. Come on, let's go."

I walked with Night through the uproar towards the door. As we went out I took one last look inside. Mebrure took a sip of champagne from her long-stemmed champagne glass and put it down. Mahmut had been dragged over to another table. The men of the Taşhan were all around him. Mahmut was lying there, half prostrate from excitement and befuddlement, breathing like a bellows. Kemal was with him.

"I understand your situation very well," he was saying. One morning years ago over at Şadırvan restaurant, I pulled a weapon on İffet. I loved her so much, and I was crazy jealous. I pulled out my gun and fired shots one after another. She fell to the floor covered with blood. I lay down on top of her. I was covered in blood. İffet died. I'll never forget that moment. I had killed her. I spent years in the Bartin Prison. I knew that I would never be able to see her again. Then I started to come to the Taşhan. I had got out of prison. My life was finished. I would sit here and drink and think about İffet. And then she came to me one night. It was incredible. She was right there in front of me. There was both pain and love in her eyes. I thought about her so much that she finally came to me.

"So now she comes every night and we sit across from each other and talk. When morning comes she goes. I understand you very well, your feelings, your behavior . . . ," he said.

İffet was standing behind. She was next to Kemal looking at Mahmut with sorrowful eyes.

Mahmut asked from where he lay, "What happened? Did she die? I killed her, didn't I?"

Kemal said, "She's sitting at her table and sipping her champagne. You didn't kill her, she's alive."

Mahmut sat up where he was and looked in that direction.

"She's sitting at the table!" he said in astonishment. "And that guy is with her. How's it possible, I pulled the trigger, I remember!"

"You can't kill an illusion, Mahmut," said Kemal.

"So I'm not a murderer?"

"No, you're not."

"Mebrure's alive."

"Yes, she's alive."

Mahmut turned silent. He was thinking of something. "Bring him a little water and let him have a drink," said Kemal. "He's all mixed up."

⇛●

We had left the Taşhan. I was walking through the streets with Night.

"What a strange thing," I murmured to myself.

"What's strange?" asked Night.

"Life. . . . People just can't get out of the rut they're in. As though nothing ever changes, everything's always the same."

"Yes, life is strange," said Night.

"My life is like that too. Everybody's is. As though we're walking along a line that's been drawn for us. Why can't people just change things?"

"Who knows. . . . Habit, fate . . . Everything's mixed together."

"Sometimes we spend our whole lives with people we randomly meet in some corner of life. Some of them stay in dreams, some of them become illusions, some of them real people. . . . Humans just can't free themselves from the same routines, they can't forget themselves; their fortunes and their fates are all mixed together. It goes on like that all life long," I said.

"Yes," said Night. "It's as though everything about a person is defined from the start; lovers, passions, death, separation, nothing really changes it. . . ."

"In a person's album there are always the same names, the same pictures," I said. "The roads in a person's memory have all been laid out, the intersections never change. What a strange thing. To love someone else, to be crazy in love with him . . . to kill him or your own self. . . ."

"What did you mean?" asked Night. He was looking intently at me.

"How do I know? . . . I'd like to be able to get outside my life for twenty-four hours. I'd like to remove myself from the past I carry in my memory and the future that's waiting for me, for twenty-four hours. For twenty-four hours, I'd like to forget my love, my expectations, my hopes, my sorrows, my habits— in short, everything that belongs to me."

"Would you like to change your place with someone else?" asked Night.

"Possibly," I said. "I'd like to change my place with someone else. So that I could get to know myself and my own life better, maybe to be more free. . . . I don't know, these are just a bunch of thoughts that cross my mind. . . ."

"Who would you like to change your life with?" asked Night.

I thought for a moment.

"With you," I said. "I'd like to change my life with you. If only that were possible."

"It's possible," said Night. "You can change places with me for twenty-four hours."

"For real?" I said. I was astonished. "I can take your place for twenty-four hours?"

"You can take my place. . . . And I'll take yours."

I was so excited.

"Okay," I said. "All those things that you manage—the darkness, events, nature—how am I going to manage them?"

"As you like . . . ," said Night.

"As I like?"

"Yes, as you like. . . ."

"And you?"

"I'll live your life for twenty-four hours."

I thought of something. "I have a violet," I said. "Take good care of it."

"Don't think about that now," he said. "Leave it to me. I'll take care of everything."

"Would you go to the Casino Venus at night? I have to teach you the machines. . . ."

Night laughed.

"I'll learn them," he said.

"Maybe you'll play the lip machine," I said. "I've been playing that in recent days. When the lips come side by side . . ."

"I know, I know . . . ," said Night.

"There are people I'm leaving whom I'm responsible for. Adviye, Celal, Irfan the Paradise guard . . . Old Gül Abla, the African violets on the table in her room . . . You must know them. . . ."

"I'll get to know them. It'll be a change for me."

"And please don't forget the Taşhan," I said. "Mebrure is there. Faruk Bey, my man . . . the illusionary women, the men who wait for them when the moon goes down . . . Bartin. . . ."

"Don't worry yourself about them," said Night.

"They can't do without me. . . ."

"I know."

I was quiet.

"When are we changing places?" I asked.

"Right now," said Night. "Are you ready?"

I was afraid, I was excited. It was no easy thing to change places with Night. I took a deep breath.

"I'm ready," I said. "My black fur is hanging in the closet. When you go to the Casino Venus, put it on. The suede high heels are on the bottom shelf. The perfumes are in front of the mirror in the bedroom. You press the third button on the right to listen to the messages on the answering machine. My African violet is in the living room; there are things to eat in the fridge, there's a pack of cigarettes or two in the bottom drawer, the key is in the inside pocket of my suede purse. The phone number for the taxi stand is written down next to the door. . . ."

"Weren't you supposed to be getting away from all these things? You weren't going to think about all these details?" said Night.

"I'm so used to it. I can't help it."

"You're giving out instructions as though you were going off on a long journey. . . ."

"I am, in a way," I said.

I began to think.

"I'm just a person," I said. "Basically just a person all by herself. I'm telling you all these things but don't pay any attention. . . ."

I was sad.

"I'm a person who's been hurt," I continued. "I hid it from you. For two months, I've been hurt. Will you be able to bear it?"

"How are you hurt?" asked Night.

"My heart is hurt. When I go to the Casino Venus in the evenings, my sadness goes away sometimes, and sometimes it gets worse. Are you going to be able to deal with this situation?"

"Maybe I'll get over it, let's see . . . ," said Night.

"You're optimistic," I said.

"Yes."

"If you can't sleep at night, drink some warm milk. That's what I do."

"You leave everything to me," he said. "Are you ready, should we change?"

"I'm ready. Let's change," I said. "You be me and I'll be you."

My heart was beating as though it would leap out of its place.

"This isn't so easy," I thought for an instant. "I am leaving behind my shell, my surroundings, my dreams, my habits, my people, what I like—In short, everything."

"What are you thinking?" asked Night.

"Nothing," I said. "Just a bunch of things. . . . So strange, it's like death. It seemed for a minute as though I were going to die, and I was describing to you the traces of the life that I was leaving behind."

"Don't think like that," said Night. "You're going to be apart from these things for twenty-four hours. Look, do you see how hard it is for someone to leave their surroundings, to break out of their cocoon?"

"Really," I said. "I have memories, they're very important. They're very important to me. Put them in a corner of your mind. Let's see if you'll be able to win on the machines. How's your luck? I'm curious. Please don't accidentally erase the messages on the answering machine."

"Don't worry about these things," said Night.

"I talk a lot, don't I?"

"No, it's very normal. You're just warm-hearted."

"You think so?"

"Yes."

"I love my violet. I love it very much. Talk to it at night," I said.

"I will," said Night. "Are we all set?"

"Yes."

At the last minute I thought of some things.

"Wait! Wait a minute," I said. "Irfan the Paradise guard may call you. Celal's his responsibility. The lot where you meet up with him is in Küçükesat, Büklüm Street, the empty place behind the grocery store. If you get cold when you're in bed, put on the black lace wool undershirt in the top drawer of the bureau. Because I had pneumonia twice, and I get cold if it snows. Absolutely don't drink the tap water. There's good water in the clay jug. The violet with the broad leaves on the table in the room with the couch in Gül Abla's apartment is her old fiancée Şakir Bey; if you should communicate with it without Gül Abla hearing, it could give you some information."

Night was laughing.

"It's like you're going on an endless journey," he said.

"Isn't it? Isn't it a little like that?" I asked.

"Or are you afraid?"

"I'm excited."

"Are you ready?"

"I'm ready."

"Then, okay," said Night.

"Just a minute!" I shouted.

I somehow couldn't get started on this trip. There were a lot of things I was leaving behind, and it was as though I couldn't separate myself from them, even for just twenty-four hours.

"Just a minute!"

"Now what?"

"If you go to the Casino Venus this evening, it might not be a good idea for you to play the lip machine. Last night the machine was closed. I mean it was just devouring chips. I don't know if it will open up tonight or not. You know, these machines have a time when they give and a time when they take. You have to get it just right. You can lose money. If two lips don't come together above the line on the first three bets, leave the machine. Go to the one with the cherries. It's at the back of the hall . . . ," I said.

"If you keep thinking about this stuff we'll never get to change places!" said Night. "And aren't you the one who wanted to forget everything for twenty-four hours?"

"I don't know . . . ," I murmured. "A person's life is something different. Now I understand this better. I can't just leave it and go. My boyfriend could call me. If he calls just when I'm not here, what would we do?"

"I'll talk to him," said Night.

"Something could go wrong. I've waited so long. If he called just when I wasn't here. . . ."

Just then the phone in my bedroom rang.

"Wait, who's this?" I said. I ran over and picked it up.

Gül Abla was on the other end. "Where were you, I was worried. You didn't come by today. You know, it's the Kandil."

I had completely forgotten that it was the Kandil.

"I'll stop by in the evening, Gül Abla," I said. I put down the phone. Turning to Night, I said, "Tonight's the Kandil. You have to go to Gül Abla's. She's expecting you; if you don't come, she'll be hurt. Get a *Kandil simidi* for her at the Körfez Pastry Shop."

"I'll get a *Kandil simidi* and go to her. Are you ready?"

"Wait," I said. "Wait a minute. I forgot to put on perfume."

Night laughed.

I went over in front of the mirror and glanced at the flasks of perfume. A million things were racing through my mind.

"Which perfume are you going to put on?"

"I don't know, I can't decide."

"The night has its own scent; anyway, what do you need perfume for?"

"Well, habit. . . . Look, you can write small notes on this yellow pad." I said. I passed it to Night.

"If you don't want to change, we can just forget about doing this . . . ," said Night.

"No. . . . Is that how I seem?" I asked.

"I don't know. You don't seem to really want to do this. You're tense. If you want, let's just forget it."

"No, no, I'm ready."

I took a deep breath.

"Come on, let's change."

"Okay," said Night. "See you right here in twenty-four hours. Forget about everything you left behind. I'll take care of everything that happens."

"See you here in twenty-four hours," I said.

I shut my eyes tight. Suddenly it seemed that huge fireworks went off in my head. Multicolored zigzag rockets, balls of light, and phosphorescent lines flew back and forth in front of my closed eyes.

I opened my eyes. I felt an indescribable lightness. I had passed over, and in an instant the time frame in which I lived, all the responsibilities I carried as a person, and all the recollections with which I had burdened my memory had simply vanished. It was as though I had been born again. A feeling of boundless freedom filled my whole being.

"It's become night," said a male voice. "Ah, ah . . . I'm sad again. It's night again."

I bent over from above and looked down. There was a drunk by the side of the road talking to himself.

All the street and avenue lights suddenly went on.

Underneath me, cities were slowly lighting up; towers, skyscrapers, shanty towns, crowded avenues, air runways, swimming pools in luxury villas, saints' tombs, fish shops, discos, fancy hotels, cooperative apartments, village coffeehouses, housing developments, intersection lights, student dormitories, ships anchored in harbors, taxis, late model cars, night clubs, street sellers of *kokoreç* with their glassed-in carts, hospitals, roller coasters, Ferris wheels reaching up to the sky, and amusement parks, all were turning on their lights.

It was an unbelievably beautiful sight. I was looking down, gazing at all these lights.

"So how are you?" I heard a voice say. I turned and looked; the full moon was poised at my left. "Are you okay? How's it going?" it asked me.

"I'm fine, I was looking at things down there," I said. "How are you?"

"I'm fine, I swear, how else should I be? Tonight's the full moon. In a little while, lovers will start to walk around arm in arm. I'm getting ready. The air is clear, basically no clouds, the stars will be out in a bit," it said. "What will you do?"

"I don't know. . . . I thought I'd just wander around a bit," I said.

"Good idea, take a walk. Go in and out of everyplace. The world is yours now," he said.

A cloud appeared. The full moon started to explain something to it.

The cloud was saying something angrily. I lent an ear.

"You can't just leave me like that. I love you. Did you forget so quickly those beautiful days we had? Or was everything you said to me just a lie?" it said.

"Stop, let's talk," said the full moon. A little later it disappeared behind the cloud.

"Hey, brother!" I called out. It slowly slipped out from behind the cloud.

"What is it, friend, did you want something?" it asked.

"Where is Ankara down there, where's Bartin? I couldn't quite pick them out, so I thought I'd ask you."

The full moon looked carefully down for a minute.

"Look," it said to me. "That's Ankara. Do you see? Let me see where Bartin is . . . There, that must be Bartin."

I looked at the places it had indicated.

Ankara was ablaze with light. I saw Anıtkabir right off. Bartin had dimmer lights, but I was still able to pick it out pretty well.

"What's that?" I said. "It's all lit up."

The full moon glanced down.

"That's Paris," it said. "That other place you see is London. Isn't it bright? And there's Berlin."

The cloud said, "Weren't you going to take me to Paris? You never did anything you promised."

"Thanks," I said to the full moon.

Now from a bird's eye view, I could see the map better from the lights underneath me. I slowly descended to Ankara.

I was in a place near Gül Abla's house. I turned into her street and went over to her apartment. I shot a look through the open window.

Gül Abla was sitting in an arm chair. The different colored African violets were on the table, in their usual place.

Night had become me, and was sitting across from her. I looked at myself from outside the window.

She was talking with Gül Abla. A package of *Kandil simitler* was lying on the table. Gül Abla took the package and went to the kitchen. She put water in the kettle from the jug and started to prepare tea.

Night bent down, and was saying something to the African violet with the broad leaves. I got really close to the window and listened to their conversation.

"Şakir Bey, Şakir Bey. . . ."

"Yes."

"How are you?"

"I'm fine thanks, and you?"

"How's Rıza Bey?"

"He's over there. Looking out the window."

"Is Cem in a good mood?"

"I'm fine, thanks," said the pale pink colored African violet from the corner.

"Our conversations always get cut off at the most exciting place," said Night. "The other day you were just about to tell me. . . ."

"Yes," said Cem. "I just couldn't give her up. I couldn't even visualize anyone else. I left my fiancée. What a woman, do you know what I mean? I could never understand how she put up with that marriage for years. I became curious about Rıza Bey, who sat quietly and calmly in the corner like a house cat. I wondered, what did this guy think about? Where and how did he meet Gül? I wondered what the first years of their marriage were like. They never had kids. Gül didn't tell me anything. It was so strange, she just closed that chapter in her life, but she kept on living with that guy. Whenever I mentioned Rıza, she just changed the topic and started to talk about something else."

The African violet with the pale pink flowers continued to talk to Night in a low voice. Gül Abla had steeped the tea in the kitchen and was pouring it into glasses with thin waists.

I slowly slipped away from there. I left them there and went straight to Bartın. First I just walked around the heights of the city. I took a quick look at the gently flowing Bartın Creek, the empty tea gardens, and the deserted Bartın Hill.

The Taşhan was in front of me. The Night Wind had come up. It was damp. It rubbed against me.

"How are you?" she said as she passed by.

"I'm fine. How's it going?" I asked.

"I'm blowing," she said. "East to west . . . Like a sailboat gently going across the sea. . . ."

"You're good," I said.

The Night Wind laughed bitterly.

"What else can I do?" she said. "Ever since I fell in love with you, ever since we got married, I've been like this. In daylight you're not here, when you do come you always go somewhere else. You just think about the stars. I could never break you away from those tarts. I never see your face."

I was listening to what the Night Wind said in astonishment.

"Are you my wife?" I asked.

"Oh, so now you've even forgot that you married me? You are too much, I swear. . . . This I'm hearing for the first time. I'm your wedded wife, did you forget?"

I couldn't even speak. I didn't know I was married, I was learning it for the first time.

"You'll go off to the stars again tonight, won't you? I'll be lonely again. I'll just blow all by myself," said the Night Wind. She started to cry.

"Which stars?" I asked.

The Night Wind, between her sobs, said, "You're so strange tonight, so different. Which stars do you think? Your mistresses. Don't you slam the door and go off to them every night? Oh, I am so unlucky. . . ."

She started to cry again.

"Are there more than one?" I asked.

"Are you fooling around with me, you?" she said. "I should ask you that. Is there just one, or are there more than one? You're never in the house. The gossip has gone all the way up to the sky. I can't even look at people. I'm going back to my father's house."

She went off. Blowing.

I was trying to think.

I heard a voice saying, "Sweetheart, I'm here. Where've you been, sweetie? I've been waiting for you." I turned and looked behind me.

There was a dazzlingly beautiful woman standing in front of me. She was blonde, with green eyes. The long evening gown that clung to her matchless body was worked with thousands of silver sequins.

At that moment I realized that I was a man. It was an incredible feeling. I looked her over from top to bottom, then looked into her eyes.

"Who are you?" I asked.

She laughed in a sexy way.

"You're always such a joker. I'm crazy about you. I'm Venus, sweetheart. You didn't forget me, did you? We were together yesterday. . . ." she said.

"Venus . . . ," I murmured.

"Yes. Your Venus."

She came over to me, and put her arms around me with the warmth of a cat. Her perfume drove me crazy. I hugged her closely.

"Not here, sweetheart. There are thousands of eyes around. Let's go to the hotel again," she said.

I put my arms around her waist. I smelled her hair, kissing her ears.

"Let's go to the hotel," she pleaded.

"Let's go."

She put her arms around my neck. We were slipping away through the air.

"Which hotel are we going to?" I asked.

"Should we go to last night's?" she asked.

"Okay. Let's go to last night's. Where was it?"

"We stayed in the Princess Hotel in Balçova in Izmir, sweetheart, did you forget?" she asked.

"Would I forget, I didn't forget. I just asked."

"Oh, you are such a joker!"

Her platinum hair was tickling my face, my neck. Her beautiful eyes were looking down, and at the same time she was kissing me.

"Where are we passing, sweetie?" she asked.

"Right now we're going from Sivrihisar towards Afyon. From there we'll go straight to Izmir above Turgutlu, we'll go into Izmir from Bornova. From Alsancak to Konak, and then from there we'll get to Balçova."

Venus clapped her hands in delight.

"It's like you're carrying me there along the highway, my love! How nice!" she said.

"Yes. I'm carrying you there above the Ankara-Izmir highway. So we'll see what it's like."

We were wrapped in each other's arms and passing above Afyon now.

"You're so unusual." Venus murmured in my ears. "If you wanted, you could take me in something like a second. But you, you're following the highway in the air. This is just wonderful!"

"I thought you'd like to see a little of things," I said.

Actually, I hadn't realized that I could go to Balçova in Izmir in an instant. I was following the highway just as I was used to doing, but from the sky!

"How long does this road take?" asked Venus.

"It takes eight hours," I said.

"How can that be?" she cried in astonishment. "Eight hours from now it will be daylight, and you'll be gone!"

I immediately corrected myself.

"What do you mean, dear, I'll speed up and we'll be there in eight minutes."

She embraced me closely around the neck again. The scent of her perfume was intoxicating.

"There's a place lit up down there!" she shouted.

I looked down. I was right above Uşak.

"Come dear," I said. "Let's go down a little here. When you pass through Uşak there's a place called the Emperor Tea Garden. Let's sit there for a little while. Let's look at the darkness. Let's look at the lights of the cars and trucks that pass in front of us on their way to Izmir. Uşak will be sleeping at our side. We'll sense that. Here we go, we're going down."

"What an unusual idea," murmured Venus. "The Emperor Tea Garden. . . . But there's no one there now. . . ."

"That's better," I said. "To sit in the middle of the night in a tea garden in Uşak in peace and quiet, to relax a little. . . ."

"You like it there . . . ," said Venus. "Who did you go there with?"

"I didn't go with anyone. Once when I was going to Izmir I saw the Emperor Tea Garden on the side of the road. . . . There were hundreds of empty chairs that seemed like they were waiting in the darkness for someone to come and sit there. The name of the tea garden touched me, too. However, it's not at all any kind of fancy place like its name. It's just a run down, long-since-forgotten, empty tea garden."

"I'm curious about it."

"Come on, we're going down," I said.

We landed in the middle of the Emperor Tea Garden.

It was dark everywhere. The tea garden was completely empty. There were tables and chairs made out of white metal scattered about. There wasn't even a flicker, any sign of life. The sign of the tea garden was lit up and then became dark with the passing lights of busses and cars on the highway.

The Emperor Tea Garden. . . .

Venus pulled out of my arms, then slowly walked around amid the tables and chairs of this lifeless tea garden.

"I've never seen a place like this before," she said. "It's so different. . . ."

"I don't think a star has ever come down here before," I said.

"How did you find it?" she asked with interest.

I said, "I told you, I was going to Izmir. The headlights of the car lit up the sign of the tea garden. I pulled my car over to the side of the road and went into the tea garden. This empty world with no people attracted me in some strange way."

We each pulled up a chair and sat at one of the tables.

The Night Wind brushed by and passed on.

"Are you cold?" I asked Venus.

"I shivered for a minute," she said.

"Your clothes are thin, let's get up."

"But I like it here."

"This is such a strange world, isn't it?" I said. "There are so many tables and chairs, but they're completely empty. This is a forgotten tea garden."

"There's no waiter either."

"There's nobody. Come on, let's go, you're cold."

Venus put her arms around my neck. We took to the air and left the Emperor tea Garden behind as we glided forward. We arrived at Bornova. Izmir was ablaze with light. From the hill, the sight of the harbor, the Kordon, and Alsancak made a person feel happy.

"It's so beautiful!" Venus shouted.

"Izmir doesn't sleep at night," I said. "Look, there's Karşıyaka, it gleams like a diamond bracelet, doesn't it? The beerhouses and tavernas along the Kordon are full to overflowing. The lights light up the bay. The traffic is passing sweetly in front of them, cars play music on their tape cassettes, lovers are in each other's arms, lonely bums have opened their bottles of *ispirito* by the seaside, waiters in the fish restaurants are carrying shrimp, *çupra*, fried mussels, octopus salad, and squid. Inside, the restaurants the belly dancers come out at this hour. They gyrate and twist in their veils as they belly dance. The drummer and piper next to a dancer get in a happy mood as she dances, and raise their *rakı* glasses in toasts from the table. When the dancer throws herself on the floor and ends the dance, the drummer strikes his drum as though he intends to smash it, the piper lifts his pipe shrilly, range upon range, as though he wants to rip apart all the sadness of the night. The restaurant rings with applause. The men stick money between the breasts of the dancer. She's a little sweaty. She bows with pleasure in every direction. Prosperous looking men roll up bills and stick them in the pipe. Look, they've lit up the Asansör. From the hill the whole bay is at their feet. Fancy cars are racing on the road that goes to Narlıdere, and Dario Moreno's house is on the street below the Asansör. A boat slips over from Karşıyaka to Pasaport. The evening tea has been brewed in the coffeehouse at Pasaport, and the waiters bring mugs of beer to those who want them. Going down from Varyant, you slide around and around in a flood of light and wind up in Konak Square. The old clock in Konak has been illuminated. So, there's Izmir beneath your feet," I said.

Venus said in admiration, "How beautifully you explain your city to me! I've never heard Izmir talked about this way."

"I like it there," I said. "The old train station, the Basmane gate of the fair, the way the girls of this hot port city like to flirt, the beds wrapped in blankets at the old Ankara *Palas* on Konak Square, the carriages touring in Güzelyalı, the old ladies who grow roses on their balconies, I like everything about Izmir. The neighborhood of Tilkilik, the gravestones that the street toughs yell at when they pass by, Three Roads, the old store that sells the belly dancers' costumes. . . ."

"You never told me anything like this before," said Venus. She was staring at me.

"I'm in a good mood all of a sudden. When I saw the city beneath me, I couldn't hold myself back. At night time, Kemeraltı is sad, all the shops are closed, and you don't hear the voices of the merchants who shout all day long. . . . Over at Basmane there are all-night coffeehouses where you can see old men who fall asleep in their chairs and pass the night. . . ."

"I understand, Izmir is your city."

"Yes, Izmir is my city. I love to live each and every street. Okay, we're going over towards Balçova. Look, you can see the lights of the Princess Hotel in the distance," I said.

The flashing lights of the Princess Hotel were visible at the end of the road. We glided down the path covered with an awning and entered through the automatic glass doors of the hotel. I said to the receptionist who was wearing glasses, "I'd like a room for the night for myself and Venus."

The receptionist looked closely at me.

"How many nights will you stay?"

"Just tonight. . . ."

"Please sign here. The room price includes breakfast. Here's your key. The casino is open to our guests," he said.

I signed the paper he held out to me.

We got into the elevator, which looked like a glass jewel box. Looking at the inner court of the hotel that was decorated with low round trees, velvet armchairs, and giant potted plants, we glided up to the top floor.

⁂

Once in bed, I couldn't fall asleep. There were a thousand thoughts passing through my brain. Venus was stretched out languorously next to me.

"What time is it?" I asked.

"I don't know, sweetheart, it must be long past midnight," she said.

"Come on, let's get dressed and get out of here," I said. "I have to be back in Ankara before daybreak."

"Why don't we do it like last night?" she murmured.

"Like what?"

"Before the dawn broke, the two of us just slowly vanished in the bed under the light. It was so beautiful. . . ."

"It was beautiful," I said. "But I have things to do tonight."

I little while later we were dressed and went down to the lobby in the glass elevator. I paid for the hotel, and we went outside.

"What will we do now?" asked Venus.

"We'll go back by the same road. Hold on to me."

She put her warm arms around my neck. She was so beautiful I didn't dare to look at her.

"Hold on tight. We don't have a lot of time, so we'll have to go quickly." I said.

She clung tightly around my neck. Slipping across the sky, I went the way of the Izmir-Ankara highway.

We went past Kula and Salihli, and we were getting close to Uşak.

"The Emperor Tea Garden. . . . It was so pretty there . . . ," said Venus. "Let's sit down there for a bit. There's still a lot of time before morning."

"Okay, we'll go down there."

The forgotten tea garden at an intersection was somehow attracting me too, with a strange fascination.

We made our way through the clouds for a while. I was slowly descending.

"Look over there!" shouted Venus.

I looked down.

A set of lights were winking at us, and in the distance, a song sung by a very unusual voice was reverberating towards us.

"What is this music? It's like somebody singing old songs. . . ." said Venus.

I recognized the voice. It was Hafız Burhan. His burning voice was rising in waves, reaching up towards us.

I was so excited, I got goose bumps.

"It's Hafız Burhan. He's singing 'Makber.'"

I was continuing the descent.

"It's so strange," I murmured. "That place lit up that we see is the Emperor Tea Garden."

"How could that be?" said Venus. When we were there it was totally empty. Everything was dark."

"Look, now it's all lit up with colored lights," I said. "The tables are full, there are lightings burning between the trees, Hafız Burhan's voice is ringing out all over the place."

We came down by the roadside. We went inside the Emperor Tea Garden, which looked like a bright ball of light in the night.

The chairs and tables that had been empty when we left a few hours earlier were now full. In astonishment, I saw that Gül Abla was sitting at the table nearest us. She had put on one of her furs that hung on the coat rack near the door. The African violets were sitting on the table. I immediately recognized Rıza Bey, Şakir, and Cem. Gül Abla had her eyes closed, listening to the incomparable refrains that Hafız Burhan was sending through the air. She didn't see us.

At one of the nearby tables, Adviye and Celal were sitting. They were looking into one another's eyes. Celal had reached out and held Adviye's hand with its lace glove. They were in their own world. Irfan the Paradise guard was sitting on a chair a little in front of them, puffing the smoke from his cigarette up into the sky. It was clear that Hafız Burhan's '*Makber*' had affected him.

I was walking hand in hand with Venus through the Emperor Tea Garden. I realized that no one could see us. At another table the African violet Faruk Bey was sitting. Mebrure was at his side. He had ordered fruit brought to the table and had them open a bottle of whiskey. Looking at Mebrure, he raised his glass and said, "Here's to you, dear."

Adviye and Celal were drinking tea in delicate glasses, clearly talking about the past and the future.

My man from the Taşhan was sitting quietly in one corner, sipping his *rakı*.

Mahmut and Meral the nurse were sitting across from one another at another table, but didn't talk very much. Mahmut had taken his head in both hands, as though the music had transported him far away. Meral the nurse was looking anxiously at him, and every once in a while stealing a glance at Mebrure, who was sitting with Faruk.

The waiter from the Taşhan was walking around, taking care of the tables.

A man sitting at one of the tables seemed very familiar. Suddenly I recognized him. It was Hadi Bey, whom I had run into at the Casino Venus. His wife was sitting across from him. Two tables away, his lover Gül was with another man. On the chair next to them I saw that there was a mink and another fur placed one on top of the other. So she had finally taken the furs from the closet.

The illusionary women slowly started to come in the gate of the Emperor Tea Garden. When I looked more carefully, I saw that the men from the Taşhan were sitting at the back tables.

The illusionary women were so beautiful . . . as though they were transparent. . . . Hafız Burhan's matchless voice was making waves in their hair, brushing past their skirts. It was going to the men, to the tables where the men were waiting for them.

"Look" said Venus next to me. "There's a beautiful stream flowing in the darkness. There are willows bending over it. That stream wasn't here before."

I turned and looked where she pointed. There was a stream softly flowing on the edge of the Emperor Tea Garden. Silent. Dark. It was Bartin Creek! I knew it right away.

"It's Bartin Creek!" I said. How strange, Bartin Creek. . . ." For a moment it seemed like I could see desolate Bartin Hill.

We were walking across the bridge above Bartin Creek now.

Suddenly my heart almost stopped with excitement. Someone was leaning against the iron balustrade of the bridge, looking at the black-flowing stream.

"What is it?" asked Venus.

"It's my man." I said. "My African violet is standing there, watching Bartin Creek go by."

"But that's not an African violet! It's a man!" said Venus. "He's just staring at the water."

"Who knows what he's thinking." I said.

"But he's not an African violet."

"No," I said. "He's a man."

We drew near. He didn't see us. He was lost in thought. I thought he seemed a little tired. I missed him so much. I kept staring at him. He looked at the water and sighed. I couldn't figure out why it was that he wasn't asleep and was out at this hour, looking at Bartin Creek.

"That's your guy? That's a man! Aren't you a man too?" said Venus.

"I'll explain later," I said.

"You're so different tonight, it's as though you've gone and somebody else has come in your place. . . ," said Venus.

"No, my dear . . . ," I said. I grabbed her tightly around the waist and pulled her towards me.

It would be dawn in a little while. The stars slowly began to fade. I glanced at Venus. She seemed tired. That brilliance she had shown the first moment I saw her was gone. Her hair seemed somehow more dull, her beautiful eyes were somehow less bright. The color of her sequined dress was worn and faded.

"I'll be back in a little while," she said. "We'll be together again tomorrow night, won't we?"

"Yes, we will," I said.

"Take me to the Emperor Tea Garden tomorrow. . . ." she murmured. "It's a strange, different kind of world there."

"Okay, I'll take you," I said.

Venus was gradually disappearing in front of me, as though she was were turning into mist and vanishing into the air.

"Don't forget tomorrow night!" she said.

She was gone.

I looked at the sky. The stars were lost.

He was still staring at Bartin Creek standing on the bridge, lost in thought.

I went over to him.

"How are you? I missed you a lot," I said.

He suddenly became irritated and turned towards me. He didn't see me. I realized he had heard my voice in the darkness. His abstracted state suddenly vanished. He looked around. He was looking for me.

"I'm here. I'm always with you. I love you," I said.

He could hear my voice, but couldn't figure out where it was coming from. I reached out and touched his cheek.

He put his hand to his cheek. He walked down off the bridge, becoming lost somewhere in the darkness.

I went back to the Emperor Tea Garden. Hafız Burhan's voice had gone silent. It was almost morning. The tea garden was completely empty. The lights in the trees were turned off, the white iron tables and chairs were scattered all over, empty. There was no one around.

I went out onto the highway. I began to run towards Ankara. The day was about to break. I would soon disappear. There was a truck in front of me. I passed it. I was running with all my strength. My lungs seemed like they would burst. I was covered with sweat. One of my shoes loosened, then flew off my foot. Now there was a tractor trailer in front of me. I passed that too.

Suddenly I saw that the sun was about to dawn behind the hills. Red clouds, the messengers of dawn, began to spread everywhere. I could hardly breathe. A sound like that from a bellows came out of my lungs. My throat was rasping.

I fell where I was in a heap. I closed my eyes.
Somewhere nearby a rooster crowed.
It was morning.

⇛₀

I lay for a while spread out on the asphalt. I didn't have an ounce of strength left, I crawled forward a little. The driver of a car coming up behind me shouted as he passed, "Are you crazy, man! You're flat out in the middle of the road, you're gonna get creamed. They'll scrape your butt off the road. Couldn't you find someplace else to narc out?"

The day had begun, in full glory. The sun rose up and the mountains and hills around me became bright.

I had no idea what to do. I had forgotten to ask Night what to do when it became day. I was looking for some place to hide, to run away to. I slowly went over to the other side of the road. I was looking to see if there was a cave, some dark place where I could hide. There were still twelve hours before I was due to meet Night. I just couldn't find a black hole. My night time freedom of movement was now very restricted. It was like my two feet were tied together; my eyes didn't see very well in the brightness, either. I looked uselessly in my pocket for my old sunglasses. Clearly I had forgotten them at home, in the chest drawer.

I thought of Venus for a minute. She was so beautiful! If I ever saw her again, I would ask her what perfume she wore. That scent enchanted me. Her shiny blonde hair, her moist lips, that sexy look in her eyes, they were all so beautiful! Who knew where she was now. . . .

Around me, everything associated with night had gone. It was as though I had been born into a different world. A world in which I couldn't get along. . . . My eyes kept looking hopelessly for night people: the tarts on the corner, the drunks, the watchmen. They were all lost and gone.

A bus stopped on the roadside. I jumped on from the back door.

"Where are you getting off?" asked the driver's assistant. He was squirting the traditional cologne into the customer's hands.

"I'll get off someplace between Afyon and Uşak. . . ."

"Let me know," said the assistant. He walked away, up towards the front.

The people on the bus had opened up the morning papers and were reading. I closed my eyes and tried to relax where I was for a while.

I opened my eyes when someone poked me. I looked; it was the assistant.

"We're at Uşak. I woke you up before we passed the place where you'll get out," he said.

"Thanks," I said. I started to look out the window.

Suddenly I saw that the intersection with the Emperor Tea Garden was just a little way in front of us. From the distance I could see the white tables and chairs.

"I'll get out here!" I called out to the assistant. The bus shook to a halt. I jumped off. The Emperor Tea Garden was in front of me. It was calm and quiet again. There was no one to be seen. I went in beneath the sign and sat down at one of the iron tables.

I looked around. The Emperor Tea Garden was very different by day. The neglect and abandonment seemed somehow more obvious. But it was still very beautiful. Very moving. It was like a place outside of this world. It sat there, empty, in the middle of four roads, as the heavy inter-city traffic coursed by.

That '*Makber*' that Hafız Burhan sang last night was so beautiful. I thought for a moment of that burning voice reverberating in the air. I drifted off.

"What would you like?" said a voice next to me.

I was startled, I opened my tired eyes. There was a waiter standing next to the table.

"What would you like?" he asked again.

"I'll have a soda," I said. "Do you have ginger ale?"

"They don't make ginger ale anymore."

"Oh, right."

"Let me bring you a *Çamlıca* soda," the waiter said.

"Fine."

Just as he was going away, I called him back.

"Yes," he said, turning around.

"I wanted to ask you something. Is there a dark place around here? You know, a nice, shady place. The sunlight, uhh, bothers me. . . ."

The waiter thought for a minute.

"There's a cinema across the way," he said. It's dark and cool.

"Is there a film on now? Is there a show? I mean, is it open?"

"It's open twenty-four hours. There's always a film showing," said the waiter. "It's actually a night cinema. If you know what I mean."

"Good," I said. "I'll go there. My eyes are bothered by the light. . . ."

"There, you go in by that side door."

"What film is showing, do you know?"

"Not exactly," said the waiter. "I can't really get away from here. It's crowded."

"It's crowded here?" I asked in astonishment.

The waiter said, "It's jammed. Not a single empty table. And I take care of all of them."

I looked closely around.

"The tables are empty. There's not a soul in the place," I said.

The waiter laughed. I saw his yellow teeth.

"All the tables are full," he said. "There's no place to even sit down. But you can't see them."

I was completely amazed.

≫•

"All of the tables are full? Who are they? Why can't I see them?" I asked.

"All the tables are full, we put extra chairs between them. Look, do you see those chairs?"

"I see the chairs. Those ones in the back, right? But they're empty like the other ones," I said.

The waiter said, "Let me bring you your soda."

"Stop, don't go," I called after him.

He turned around, looking at me.

"Are those tables really all full?"

"What did I tell you, they're completely full. There's no place to sit. They're calling me," said the waiter. He stuck his pen behind his ear and went off.

I didn't know what to think.

My soda came.

I took a sip, looking at the empty tables and chairs around me.

The waiter was moving quickly among the empty tables, taking care not to bump into the chairs that were around them, writing down some orders on the pad in his hand.

I signaled with my hand and called him over. He slipped between the tables masterfully and came over to me.

"Did you want something else?" he asked.

"You're very busy," I said. "You keep writing down orders."

"Yes," said the waiter. "There are a lot of orders. What can I bring you?"

"Bring a glass of tea," I said. "Wait, don't go right away. I want to ask you something."

"Go ahead," he said. At the same time his eyes were combing the Emperor Tea Garden. He called out to a distant table, "I'll be right over."

"Is it always this full in this tea garden?"

"It's always like this," said the waiter. At night it's even more crowded. With your permission, they're calling me from that other table, let me take their order."

He started to move around amid the tables again.

I sat in my chair in the middle of all the empty tables and chairs in the Emperor Tea Garden, and watched the waiter run from table to table.

"You seem tired. I haven't seen you here before. Do you come often to this tea garden?" a male voice asked. I turned and looked in the direction of the voice. The table there was empty, there was no one there.

The voice continued to speak.

"I'm here, I'm sitting next to you at this table. Would you like a cigarette?"

I saw in astonishment that there was a pack of Marlboro cigarettes hovering in the air near me.

"Light one up. For God's sake, go ahead. It'll relax you," said the voice.

I took a cigarette from the pack in the air and put it to my lips.

An old fashioned gas lighter lit up in the air, then slowly reached over and lit up my cigarette. It was like an illusion. Like a trick done by a master magician.

Both the lighter and the pack of cigarettes had now disappeared.

I took a drag on the cigarette in my hand. I looked in confusion at the empty table next to me from which the sound had come.

"It's very crowded here, isn't it?" I asked. Just to say something. . . . You know. . . .

The voice said, "It's not too bad this morning. Sometimes you can't even find a place to sit down. You wind up having to share a table with someone you don't even know. But look, what you said is true. There are people here. It's gradually filling up, the garden. You're right," he answered me.

"Yes, the garden's getting more and more crowded," I murmured.

I let my eyes wander around. The sun was well up in the sky. There was absolutely no one to be seen in the Emperor Tea Garden.

"Look, look, the General's here too," said the voice.

My eye went to the empty table across from me. There was a brown cane with a brass handle resting on the edge of the chair.

The waiter dashed over to that table.

"He comes to the garden every morning at the same time, the General," said the voice. "He has his orderly with him. Look, he's opened his thick notebook and taken out his pen. The General's writing down his memoirs. He dictates, and the orderly writes it down."

I looked closely at that table.

There was a thick notebook open on the table now. In the middle, where the pages separated, a pen was resting.

"They start when they drink their tea," said the voice. The waiter brought two teas to the table. Two thin-waisted tea glasses stood next to one another on the table. I saw that a lump of sugar was put in each of them.

I followed the events taking place as though hypnotized.

Two silver spoons appeared in the air, and began to stir the sugar in the glasses. A little later the tea glasses rose in the air, and went straight towards mouths I could not see. The tea inside grew less, mouthful by mouthful.

"It's an illusion!" I said. "It's unbelievable. What I just saw reminded me of the tricks of the great illusionist Salvano and the *Shimada* of Japan."

"Did you say something?" said the voice.

"The General is drinking his tea," I said.

"Yes, the General and his orderly are sipping their tea," he said.

"Do you know the General?"

"I know him from here, from this garden. He comes every day. I believe his memoirs are largely done. Look, the General has started to dictate. The orderly is writing down what he says."

A new page was open on the notebook sitting on the table. A black pen was quickly writing something in invisible sentences.

"And the orderly's handwriting is beautiful," said the voice. "He's writing it like the *Sülüs* style. The tails of some of the letters are very long. . . ."

"Has he been with the General for a long time?"

"I believe they've been together for many years. The General's right leg is artificial."

"Really?" I said with surprise.

"Yes," said the voice. "Shrapnel tore it to pieces in the war. You can't even tell it's a prosthesis, can you? He uses a cane."

"I know," I said. "His cane is over there. I saw it. It's hanging on the chair."

"Yes. A cane with a brass handle. Very elegant, isn't it?"

The tea in the thin-waisted glasses was finished. The waiter took the empty glasses and refreshed the tea.

"See, she's come too, she's sitting at the table," said the voice.

"Who?" I asked with interest. I was looking at the tables around me at the same time.

"Madame Kelebek." said the voice. "The woman the General's in love with."

A black suede evening bag worked with gleaming black sequins had been placed on the table next to me.

"Madame Kelebek?"

"Yes. One of the old White Russians. She's so beautiful, isn't she? In a minute she'll lift the tulle veil from her face. Then take off her hat. Madame Kelebek. She's always in priceless furs. She's come here in the clothes that she goes to the opera in. . . ."

An unfamiliar perfume smell came to my nostrils. The voice seemed to read my thoughts. "Madame Kelebek's perfume," he said. "It must be a top quality French scent . . . it reached to the General."

A long thin silver cigarette holder appeared. For a while it just remained there motionless in the air. A platinum cigarette box gleamed in the sun like a mirror. Then it slowly opened, and a cigarette was selected from it and put into the tip of the cigarette holder.

The waiter seemed to fly between the tables, and lit the cigarette in the tip of the holder.

A drag was taken from the cigarette holder, and a puff of smoke blew into the air.

A single black glove appeared on the table. It was a long evening glove. On it was a gleaming bracelet with rubies and diamonds. When I looked more closely, I noticed that the rubies made the body of a butterfly and the diamonds its two open wings.

The glove expertly took the silver cigarette holder out of the air and flicked its ashes into the ashtray on the table.

The pen swiftly writing in the notebook on the General's table paused. It remained waiting there.

"Ah!" said the voice next to me. "The General is confused now. Madame Kelebek is in front of him. The writing stopped. It's always like this. When Madame Kelebek comes and sits in her place in the tea garden, the General loses his concentration. The orderly stops scribbling down everything he says."

What I saw and witnessed were simply unbelievable. Now I couldn't take my eyes off Madame Kelebek's table.

The waiter had brought gold champagne in a crystal glass to Madame Kelebek's table on a tray. The velvet glove reached out and took the crystal glass with its long, thin stem. It brought it to the lips I could not see.

"She has a sip or two of champagne every morning," said the voice. "She's a strange woman, Madame Kelebek. She's very attractive, isn't she? The lace veil covering her face is opening slowly."

A red lip print appeared on the rim of the champagne glass.

I thought for an instant of the machine with the lips I tirelessly played in the Casino Venus, where I waited for the two red lips to appear next to one another above the line.

There at that time of the morning in the Emperor Tea Garden as I watched a whole series of incredible events, I was so far removed from that world. . . .

My eyes were on the champagne glass left on the table, with the lip print on the rim.

"So the General is in love with Madame Kelebek?" I asked.

"He's madly in love with her," said the voice.

"Did they meet in this tea garden?"

"I don't think so. I imagine they met one another many long years ago."

"I wonder if Madame Kelebek shares the General's feelings."

"Who knows," said the voice. "Madame Kelebek is a sexy lady. Unusual . . . If she weren't interested, she wouldn't come and sit here every morning."

"Don't they ever talk?"

"No, they never talk. I've never heard of their speaking. They just look at one another."

"Interesting . . . ," I said.

"They speak with their eyes, that's a strange thing . . . ," said the voice.

A single eye appeared above Madame Kelebek's table. It was a misty eye, carrying the traces of a busy night, looking sensual under its long lashes. It was staring as a panther would stare at its prey.

"Madame Kelebek's eye . . . ," I whispered.

"Yes," said the voice. "It's looking at the General."

I looked at the General's table. A single eye had appeared in the air there as well. It was a dark eye, sunken in its place, with a fierce glare. I saw immediately that there were storms inside, a thousand feelings.

"The General's eye," I said.

"Yes, they're looking at one another, see . . . ," said the voice. "There's an incredible energy between them, do you feel it? It's like electricity, very powerful."

Now over by Madame Kelebek's table, a mouth with red lips appeared a little below the eye. The lips took a drag from the mouthpiece. The eye became even more sensual.

Excitedly I said, "Madame Kelebek's face is appearing little by little!"

"It won't all appear, just this much."

"You see her, don't you?"

"Yes," said the voice.

My eyes were fascinated by the lips. It was as though they were the lips from the machine I played on my lonely nights at the Casino Venus.

I suddenly realized the eye was looking at me. I was eye-to-eye with Madame Kelebek's single eye now. The red lips moved.

"She's saying something to you," said the voice. "But I've never seen her speak to anyone else before."

It was a smoky voice. "Where did you come from to here, to this garden?" she asked me.

"Did you ask me something, Madame Kelebek?" I said in excitement.

"Yes. I wondered where you came from to this garden."

"I came from the Izmir highway," I said.

"Oh, really . . . ," said the lips. The black velvet glove reached out to the champagne glass, and brought it to her lips.

Madame Kelebek took a sip from her champagne. Her misty eyes bearing the traces of the night turned to the General again. The General's single eye that was visible was on Madame Kelebek's eye.

"There they are, eye-to-eye again," said the voice. "There's such an incredible electrical current between them, can you feel it?"

"I feel it," I murmured. "It's love. This electrical current is love itself."

"It really is," said the voice. "Why didn't I ever think of that before? It's the electricity of love. . . ."

The waiter appeared amidst the tables. He was carrying a tray with cups full of *salep* on it. He was walking quickly around the Emperor Tea Garden, leaving the *salep* at the empty tables.

He was passing between the General and Madame Kelebek's table now. Suddenly he gave a scream, tossed his tray into the air and flew off into a corner. The waiter was bent in two, writhing on the ground. He face was purple, his whole body began to shake. His mouth was foaming a little, and his eyes were popping out.

The voice next to me began to shout in excitement.

"Something happened to the waiter! We have to do something. He went into the electrical current between Madame Kelebek and the General. The tray in his hand must have attracted the electricity. The poor think is just twisting around! He's trying to save himself. . . ."

I bent down and tried to hold the waiter by his arms. I wiped the foam from his lips with my handkerchief. His eyes looking at me were filled with horror.

"Wait!" I said. "Let me push you a little to this side. Help me. Pull in your legs. Let me get you out of this current."

The voice was shouting. "He's stuck there, he can't move! What can we do?"

I turned towards Madame Kelebek's table.

"Madame" I said. "Would you close your eye for a minute? The poor waiter got caught in the electrical current between you and the General. I can't get him out of it. His heart may not be able to take it. Would you please close your eye? So the electricity will stop. Otherwise I won't be able to help him."

The eye at Madame Kelebek's table slowly closed.

The waiter immediately felt better. From his forehead and temples, sweat was pouring in streams onto his neck. His face was completely yellow. He took a deep breath. His trembling lessened and then stopped. He came to himself.

"What happened to me?" he murmured.

"You went into the electrical current between Madame Kelebek and the General. The metal tray in your hand attracted the electricity," I said.

"What an odd thing," said the waiter.

"Yes. That powerful vibration between two people we call love, that electrification, gave you a shock."

"It knocked me for a loop," said the waiter. "I thought I was dying. Once when I was a kid I got malaria. It was like that."

I took the waiter's arm walking over towards the kitchen in the back corner of the Emperor Tea Garden.

"Let me sit inside in the shade for a bit," said the waiter. "My legs won't hold me up. It's like my whole body has gone dead on me."

The voice was right next to us. It had come along with us.

"So if you fall crazy in love, you won't be able to take it and you'll pass away," it said to the waiter.

"Love?" murmured the waiter. His eyes went off in the distance for a minute. He stretched out on a wooden bench over by the kitchen. His sweaty white shirt stuck to his scraggly body; his hair was mussed up.

"You said love, didn't you?" he asked from where he lay. "Love. I understand. I understand that at that instant I was caught in another love. How strange. . . ."

"You got caught in the love electricity between two completely other people," I said. "You're not the one who's in love. . . ."

"Ah!" the waiter laughed bitterly. "But I remembered that feeling. I know it. I know love. I lived it years ago. . . ."

His eyes drifted off to the ceiling of the kitchen. His face changed, and suddenly became as innocent as a child's face.

"Did you love her a lot?" I asked.

"And how . . . ," sighed the waiter. "It's like I suddenly went back to those days. Sometimes I have that feeling, that pain I felt, that happiness I experienced all night long in my dreams. The fragments, the traces left in my mind . . . they're such strange dreams. I saw her once in my dreams. Years later. For days I wandered around the tea garden like a sleepwalker. Among the tables, like I had been beaten up. . . ."

"Was it a long time ago?" I asked.

The waiter turned his eyes on me. His look was sad.

"A long time ago. A very long time ago. I wasn't working in the Emperor Tea Garden then. I hadn't met any of these people yet. I was young, you know what I mean? I didn't know anything about life, love, obsession. I fell deeply into love like you fall into the sea. I didn't know what to do. I was struggling in that endless water. But now . . . now I know everything. Since I started working in the tea garden I've heard, seen, and learned everything. But unfortunately, she's not in my life anymore. And I've become old, too. . . ."

A deep silence filled the kitchen.

"Was she pretty?" I asked softly.

The waiter turned his eyes to me again.

"Wouldn't she be? Of course she was very beautiful," he said. His eyes were moving silently where he lay, as though he were saying something to himself that I could not hear.

"Are you okay?" I asked.

"I'm fine, I'm fine. I've come to myself," he said.

He had sat up straight on the bench now.

"The customers outside are waiting for me," he said. "I'm behind on the orders."

"Rest a little, pull yourself together," I said.

The waiter was thinking about something where he sat.

"You know," he said, "It's so strange . . . I want to go into that electrical current again."

I was amazed.

"You almost died, I could hardly get you out of there. What do you mean, you'd go back in that current again?" I asked.

"I was dying, but I felt that I was living. It's a weird thing. I went back to that time long ago I told you about. I felt her next to me. A person lives through something like that only once. It was like all those feelings that I had lost, that I had suppressed, were alive again. . . . I'm going to go in that current again," he said. He got up. He seemed determined.

"Like electroshock therapy," I said.

The waiter went out into the garden and found the tray that had rolled away.

"I'm ready. I'm going into the electric current. Stay near me," he said.

He was walking towards the tables where Madame Kelebek and the General were sitting.

I glanced in that direction. The eyes at the tables were looking at one another again. The voice was next to me. "It's crazy, what this waiter wants to do. This time we may not be able to save him, he could die," he said.

"What can I do, it's what he wants."

The waiter was walking slowly with the tray in his hand, trying to catch the line between the two eyes. He turned to me.

"I couldn't get it," he said. "I couldn't get into the current. I'll try again."

He held the tray in his hand up to the sun now. He was right between the two tables. Suddenly he screamed and fell to the ground.

"He went into the current!" said the voice.

The tray flew from his hand. His eyes had bulged out from their sockets, he was trembling. The waiter was struggling and kicking on the floor.

"He's dying!"

"He's living the love he lost at the same time. That's why he went into the current again."

I watched the waiter writhing on the floor for a while. His lips had started to turn purple. Strange rasping noises were coming from his mouth.

"That's enough," said the voice. "He may not be able to take any more."

I went over to the waiter and grabbed his flailing arms.

"I'm pulling you out of this electrical current. You can't take any more."

The waiter was talking in gasps.

"I slept with her. I slept with her. It was so beautiful!" he said. His eyes turned on me like the eyes of a dying man. With one pull I got him out of the current.

"You were dying!" I said.

He was covered with sweat. The color gradually came back to his yellow face.

"It was so fantastic!" he murmured. "It was like a dream. I mastered her. She was in my arms. I felt her breath on my face, on my eyes."

The voice said, "He's doing it with the lover he lost in the electric current. It's very dangerous. He'll start to do it every day. . . ."

"Well, you know best."

The waiter got to his feet, straightened himself up, found his pen, and put it behind his ear.

"Have to look after the customers," he said. "I'm going to take the orders. New people have come."

Now he started to move quickly among the empty tables in the Emperor Tea Garden.

"That electrical current," I said the voice next to me. "Now I wonder what it's like to go in there. What do you experience, what do you feel? I'm going to go into the electrical current, too. . . ."

"Please," said the voice anxiously. "Who's going to rescue you from there? Don't do it, please don't do it. You have to think carefully before you take a step like that. You could remain there forever."

"Yes, I could remain forever in the electrical current between the looks of Madame Kelebek and the General. I'm going in," I said.

"You've made up your mind. . . . You'll go into that dangerous space. . . ."

"I'm going in. I want to know what the waiter experienced."

"Are you the same as the waiter?"

"I don't know. I'll see right now. All right, I'm going."

I took a step towards that strange electric line between Madame Kelebek and the General that we call love.

My whole body shook. I had plunged into the electrical current at my first step. For a minute it seemed as though I couldn't breathe, as though my heart would stop.

I was running madly through a dark tunnel. I wasn't quite sure whether I was running from someone or to get to someone. I was inside a whirlpool, a maelstrom; my heart was pounding with excitement. For an instant I felt limitless happiness. I thought: what if the tunnel had no end, what if I just stayed here. I felt that someone was calling to me.

"I'm here," I shouted. My childhood, my adolescence, my hopes, my disappointments; they were all mixed up together. Dream and reality had all floated into one another, like the design on a marbleized paper. It was as though I had taken a very powerful stimulant. My soul was naked, my heart was exposed. Anyone could touch it and take it into their hand. I was running and stopping. I heard the voice calling me again.

"Where are you? You're late. I worried about you. What did you do?" asked Night.

I was in my room. I was lying in my bed.

"I experienced unbelievable things . . . ," I murmured.

He was looking at his watch.

"It's time for us to change. We were supposed to meet here twenty-four hours later, and the time is up," he said.

"That was so quick," I exclaimed. I was astonished. "You mean it's been twenty-four hours since we changed places?" I said.

"Did you meet Venus?" he asked.

"I did. She's a fabulous woman."

Night laughed like a rascal.

"I love her," he said. "What did she tell you?"

"She didn't tell me very much. We didn't have much time. I took her around."

"Where did you take her?"

"I took to Izmir over Ankara, Uşak, and Turgutlu."

"Did you take her by the highway?"

"Yes."

"Why?"

"I like that road . . . ," I said. "Do you know the Emperor Tea Garden?"

"The Emperor Tea Garden? I never heard of it. Where is it?" he asked.

"It's in Uşak, by the side of the road, at the intersection, an old, abandoned tea garden."

"I don't know . . . I must have seen it, but I didn't notice it, I guess," he said. "What's there?"

I thought for a second.

"It's hard to explain," I said. "There's the waiter, empty tables and chairs, a cane with a brass handle that belongs to an old General tossed on one of the chairs; an evening bag worked with sequins that belongs to a sexy lady; the champagne glass that she raised to her lips; an electrical current that formed along the line where the two of them looked at one another . . . In other words, the line of love and passion. . . . There's everything in it! The waiter accidentally crossed the line, then made love to the lover he lost years ago while fighting and struggling in the current; he went back and forth between life and death. . . . He was diving into the line—in other words, into the current—so that he could live it just once again, even at the cost of his life. . . . Everything's in there!"

Night was listening very carefully to what I said.

"The Emperor Tea Garden," I murmured. "Empty tables full of invisible people, that strange abandonment, neglect. The physical expression of an emotional current, of sexuality expressed in its most powerful form between two people looking at each other. . . . The waiter suddenly got hold of his past . . . he was telling me in a childlike way of what he had felt and experienced. . . . I'll go there again."

Night was deep in thought again.

"What are you thinking about?"

"The Emperor Tea Garden. . . . Do you think it's really in this world?"

"It is in this world. I told you I was just there a little while ago."

"I hope you'll be able to find it again . . . ," said Night.

"Why shouldn't I find it?"

"What you said were strange things. . . ."

"I'm going there."

"I'm coming too."

⇒●

When we came to the intersection, I jumped out from the bus. Night had fallen, and the sky was filled with stars. I took a breath of the night air and looked around.

The Emperor Tea Garden lay in front of me. I walked under its old sign and entered the garden.

The garden was empty, as always. A cricket chirped in the distance and was silent. I started to walk among the empty tables and chairs.

The waiter appeared beside me.

"Welcome," he said. "Please, sit down. The garden is dark. The moon is behind the clouds. I'll bring candles to the tables. I'm getting them ready inside."

"Is it very crowded?" I asked.

"It's a summer night. It's packed," said the waiter. "I don't know if I have enough candles."

Now he was going about among the tables, lighting the candles he had placed with the matches he had in his hand.

There was an incomparable picture before my eyes. In the garden that lay in darkness, there were hundreds of candles burning on the tables. On some of them the flames were trembling, some of them were as still as a drop of water.

I looked at the scene for a while.

"How is it?" asked the waiter next to me. "It turned out nice, didn't it?"

"Like a dream . . . ," I murmured. "So beautiful."

"I'm glad you like it," said the waiter. "Let me take the orders."

"Are the customers from the daytime still here, or did they go?"

"Some of them left, and there are some new ones. . . . Lots of people come and go in this garden."

"Did Madame Kelebek and the General leave?"

"No, they didn't go. They're still sitting where they were."

I heard voice near me.

"I'm still here," it said. "The weather's so beautiful, I stayed here in the garden and didn't go anywhere. . . ."

"Isn't Madame Kelebek going to the opera this evening?"

"She'll still go, but much later, probably," said the voice. "She's still sitting at her table."

In the candle light, I saw the black evening bag worked with sequins resting on the table.

"And the General?" I asked.

"He's there too, sitting at the table with his orderly. They closed the notebook, and I think they've finished writing for the day."

The waiter came to my table.

"There's hot *salep*. Should I bring some?" he asked

"All right, I'll have some," I said. I called after him, "Wait, don't go!"

He turned around, and stood near me.

What happened to that electric current, that line between their eyes?" I asked. "At night time it's lost, maybe it's gone altogether. . . ."

"It's never lost," he responded. "The current gets more powerful at night. You know, desire gets stronger. . . ."

"But how can they look at one another in the darkness?"

"They look at one another by candle light. See what I mean. . . ."

When I looked very closely I could see the two eyes looking at one another.

The waiter explained.

"Now everything's slower, softer. We're far away from the blazing light of day. Darkness and candlelight slow everything down, make it softer. If a person goes into this current at night he could experience very different things, and not be so shaken up," he said.

"So did you go in the current again?"

"A little while ago," said the waiter. His voice suddenly changed, as though he were in a daydream.

"I was with her again," he said. "She was waiting for me. She knew I would come again. This time I dived in like I was letting myself go into the water of a river. Everything was a little different. The General doesn't see well at night. Because of his age. So I dove slowly into that world. Everything seemed a little calmer, a little quieter. My girlfriend was sitting on the edge of the bed. The satin light-rose pillows she had embroidered for her trousseau were at the head of the bed. This time I slowly lay down beside her. I caressed her as I had wanted to for years. Her face, her hair. . . . 'Should I light the light?' she asked me. 'Don't light it, it's better like this . . . ,' I said. I didn't want her to see that I had aged. She knew me when I was a young guy. I had thick hair then, I used to comb it back with lemon. . . ."

"Didn't she get any older?" I asked.

"No, she was just like when I last saw her. . . ." said the waiter. "She was just around twenty-one. Memories don't age . . . ," said the waiter. He ran his hand through his thinning hair.

"It's so strange, I missed her right away," he said. "Let me serve the *salep,* and I'll come back to you. I miss her so much, I can't get my fill, do you know what I mean? Let me give out the *salep* and I'll be back," he said.

I sat in the Emperor Tea Garden that was illuminated by candlelight as though I were in a dream.

The waiter came over to me again.

"I'm going into the current," he said. "I'm going to meet her. On the bed, with the satin ruffles. . . ."

He was trying to make out the line of vision between the General and Madame Kelebek.

"If the General falls asleep, I'm finished," he said.

"What happens then?"

"What do you think, everything gets stuck. The General sometimes falls asleep at night in the open air. I'd better go right away."

He made it into the line. He slowly collapsed to the floor as though diving into a dream. His eyes were half-open. There was a happy smile on his lips.

"He's gone," said the voice. "He's gone to his lover."

I sipped the *salep* he had brought me. The waiter was spread out on the floor, just lying there. Like the happiest person in the world.

The voice said, "Oh my God! The General's head nodded. He's started to sleep!"

I looked at the waiter. He slowly began to struggle anxiously from where he lay on the floor. He sighed deeply and turned on his side. He reached out his right hand as though he were trying to touch something unseen. Suddenly he opened his eyes. He slowly got up from where he was. Brushing the dust from his back he came over to me.

"What happened?" I asked.

"Everything stopped in the middle," he said. "Everything stopped in the middle. I took her in my arms. She was about to be mine. Her unique perfume filled my nostrils. I was trembling with excitement and desire. I quickly helped her undress. I brushed my cheek with the satin pillow in the darkness. I was burning with desire. Suddenly I felt that everything had just slid away and vanished from within my hand. It was an awful feeling. Her tiny firm breasts just disappeared from the palm of my hands. I realized something had gone wrong. That world, my lover, the bed, the ruffles . . . they had all disappeared. I found myself lying on the earth."

"The General fell asleep," I said.

"I know, I know that's what happened. . . ." said the waiter. "The current was cut. I fell outside of things."

He looked around disconsolately.

"He'll sleep until morning," he said.

"What'll you do?"

"That's it for tonight. That current won't come any more. I can't go in. Madame Kelebek will get up in a little while. She'll go to the opera."

"You'll wait for tomorrow morning," I said.

"You know, I got used to being close to her, now it's going to be hard to wait. . . ." said the waiter. "And I wonder if I'll be able to find that world tomorrow. Will everything be the same? That bed, those satin pillows, her hair spreading down over her shoulders . . . or was everything set up for me to experience it just today?"

"We'll know tomorrow," I said.

The candles on the table would tremble, then either flare straight up or remain burning motionlessly.

"There are people who've come," said the waiter. His eyes were burning like coals. "You think I'll be able find that world again tomorrow, what do you say?"

He was upset. He went quickly around the tables and came back to me.

"The candles are about to finish," he said. "The garden will be buried in darkness in a little while. If we could wake the General up. If we could wake him up, that would take care of everything. They'd start to look eye to eye again. I would go inside the current. If we could wake up the General before the candles go out. . . ."

"How can I wake up someone I've never met or seen?" I asked. "He's obviously tired out, he's fast asleep."

"We have to do something, we have to wake him up," said the waiter. "The candles are about to go out. Everything may not be the same tomorrow, do you understand? I have to live this tonight."

"Say a little something," I said. "Maybe he'll wake up."

"Maybe . . . ," said the waiter. He raised his voice a little. "General, General!" he called out.

The single closed eye at the General's table opened.

"He's a soldier, you know, light sleeper," said the waiter. "General!" he called out again.

The General opened his eye and looked around.

He caught Madame Kelebek's eye.

"They're looking at each other!" whispered the waiter. "Let me dive into the electric current between them before the candles go out."

"Wait a little, the General's still half asleep," I said.

"There isn't much time," said the waiter. He was excited. "The candles might go out at any moment."

He slowly walked and went into the line formed by the General's and Madame Kelebek's glances. He moaned softly and fell to the floor.

The voice next to me said, "He went into the current. He's gone to be with his lover."

The waiter was just lying there on the floor beneath the trembling light of the candles. That limitless happiness I had seen before appeared on his face. His eyes were half open. He was moaning softly.

"He found the world," I said. "But the candles on the table are about to go out."

"Beautiful things don't last long," said the voice. "People can never get their fill of them."

I glanced at the waiter curled up on the floor.

In the darkness, people began to appear at the tables that had been empty till then. With a strange fear, I saw that the garden buried in darkness was really completely full. The last candle flickered and went out. I saw in the darkness that the Emperor Tea Garden was very crowded.

"Are you afraid?" said the voice next to me. I turned and looked, the owner of the voice: Recep, my classmate from the Evliya Çelebi Primary School I had attended years ago on the slopes of Kasımpaşa.

"Recep!" I cried.

"Have I changed?" he asked.

"You've changed. But I knew you right away. So you're the one who's always right next to me in this garden."

"I was with you" said Recep.

"What are you looking for in this garden?" I asked. Recep ran his fingers through his salt-and-pepper hair that I could barely make out in the darkness.

"Most of us come to this garden," he said. "We sit here, take the sun, have a tea or coffee, watch the life flowing quickly by on the highway. Those trucks, busses, private cars, going from city to city. . . ."

A strange shiver passed through me. A cool night breeze brushed my body and passed on.

"Are you alive, Recep?" I slowly asked.

"I'm not," he said. I had figured it out.

"For a long time."

"It's been awhile."

"Okay, and the General? Madame Kelebek?"

"They lived and died a long time ago," said Recap.

I was astonished.

"But that electric current between them, that love?"

"That love is alive. Strong feelings like that don't die!"

"Well, the waiter?"

"The waiter's alive. He's living," said Recap.

"Most of the people in the garden. . . ."

"Yes."

We didn't talk any more.

The waiter opened his eyes, and sat up where he was.

"Did you find your friend?" I asked.

"I found her, I found her. . . . She was waiting for me. She was sitting in the middle of the light-rose cushions, her hair down around her shoulders. If you knew how beautiful . . . ," he murmured. I had just taken her in my arms, and I was undoing the buttons on her nightgown. It was a print with big flower sprays on it. She was snuggling close to me. He body was so hot. What an incredible thing. I touched her naked breast slowly with my hand. She moaned. And then I found myself here on the ground. Like they pulled me away from her, away from that world."

Recep said, "The candles in the garden went out. The current between the general and Madame Kelebek was buried in the darkness."

The waiter murmured, "I understand. I have to wait for tomorrow morning. I come and then I go. She's confused too. Just when I take her in my arms, I disappear. She's waiting there on the bed. As soon as I come I go. To make sure that everything is real, I bury my face in the satin pillows every time I come. Well, anyway, I should start the service. My life's always like this, run here, run there. . . ."

He walked off towards the kitchen with rapid steps.

Recep and I were there together. My eyes were combing the tables at the Emperor Tea Garden now. They were quite used to the dark. I could see who was sitting there now.

"Recep, I wonder if my mother is here; does she know about the Emperor Tea Garden? Does she come in here once in a while?" I asked.

"Your mother's here," said Recep.

For a moment I thought my heart would stop from excitement.

"My mother's here? Well, where?"

"She's sitting at one of the back tables. Come on, I'll take you to her," Recep said.

I had never felt as I felt then in all my life. My heart was beating as though it would burst, my hands were trembling with excitement. I wanted to laugh and I wanted to cry.

"Come," he said, "Let's go between those tables."

As I walked behind him, we passed between the crowded tables. Those sitting there were like yellowed photographs looking out at me from an old photo album. Some of them had on very unusual old-fashioned clothes; their hair was done in a different way; the women had thin eyebrows, and a different kind of makeup. Some of them were in very modern clothes; old and young, male and female, all mixed up together; a big crowd. They were sipping *salep* and chatting with one another. I was following behind Recep. It was as though my heart had wings, my knees were shaking.

I suddenly saw my mother. She was sitting at a table near the kitchen. There was a porcelain cup in front of her, as always. She had seen me. She got up laughing.

"Mommy!" I was able to say. I couldn't speak, there was something stuck in my throat.

"Come, sit by me," said my mother.

She had on the jacket she wore when she went to the Hilton Hotel, with a silk scarf around her neck. I saw her green eyes looking at me with love from behind her eyeglasses.

"The last time I saw you was in the hospital, in the bed, Mommy," I said. "When I got there you were in a vegetative state. You have no idea how much I've missed you."

"Don't cry, there's nothing to cry about. Look, we're together again," my mother said.

"It's like a nightmare has been ripped into shreds. I can't believe it, I can't believe that I found you again," I said.

The waiter was next to us. My mother ordered a cup of tea for me as well.

"Sit down there across from me, let me see you a little. How are you? What are you doing? How's your health? Are you happy, my child?" she asked.

"Right now I'm the happiest person in the world, Mother," I said. "I never considered that I'd be able to find you in the Emperor Tea Garden."

"I'm here, my child," said my mother. "I like this back table. I drink my tea, and see what's going on. How are you?"

"I'm fine," I said. For some reason I was out of breath. As though I had run for a long time through some place and got to my mother that way.

"How's your life?" asked my mother.

"I'm living through a lot of things, Mommy," I said. "I have so many things to tell you, I don't know where to start."

"I know," she said. "I know most of it."

"I'm writing a new book."

"You're in good spirits, that's clear. I understood that you were writing. . . ."

"I'm in love with someone. He's a very good person, Mother," I said. "A friendly, happy person. I just realized that this is a very important thing."

"It's a good thing the person you love is friendly and happy," said my mother.

"I've been going to casinos lately. I like the different game machines they have there."

My mother laughed.

"You always liked to play with toys. You were always passionate. But at least, don't lose any money . . . ," she said.

"There are different machines, Mother. The latest model Japanese game machines. Maybe they take away people's loneliness. They soak up loneliness like a sponge and take it away. I thought a lot about where their irresistible attractiveness comes from. The machines are like magnets. You have no idea."

"I don't," said my mother. "I never saw those machines. When I was young, I used to like to play card games. Later I gave that up, too."

"I know, your bridge table is in my living room in Ankara now. You know the one that opens and closes, with the green baize middle. I had it varnished. It's folded up. There are photographs on it, photographs taken on my last birthday. A mother of pearl sea shell . . ."

"Photographs taken on your last birthday," said my mother. "You went around Ankara that night with him, didn't you? You went up the Tower. You leaned against the concrete wall in the darkness and looked down from the hill at the streets, the shanty towns you could see from far away, the taxis and busses like toys in the streets. Then you wanted to go to the amusement park whose lights you could see in the distance. You went down from the tower and took a taxi together to the amusement park. There was a huge gondola decorated with lights and filled with people swinging back and forth in the air. You looked at the bumper cars and watched the Ferris wheel go up to the sky. The corn vendors were selling ears of corn, and there was an idle crowd roaming around. You were as happy as a child to be there with him."

In amazement I asked, "Mommy, how do you know all this?"

"I know," said my mother laughing.

I hugged her. I put my head on her shoulder and breathed in that smell that I missed so much; I wanted this moment to never end.

The waiter came over to us.

"There's fresh *salep*. Should I bring some, Şermin Hanım?" he asked my mother.

"Bring it, Necati," said my mother. "Bring one for my daughter too. Lots of cinnamon."

"You got it."

"Necati," said my mother. "You seem tired. Are you sick, my boy?"

The waiter took a breath.

"I've been experiencing some very unusual things during the last twenty-four hours, Şermin Hanım," he said. "I go over to the other side, I come back to this one. You understand. . . . I found Hatice. The girl I love. After I looked for her all these years. . . ."

"Tired from love, how nice . . . ," said my mother. "Make sure you don't lose Hatice, Necati."

"You think I'd lose her?" said the waiter. "I'd do anything I could not to lose her."

"When you find love you mustn't let it go," said my mother. "Otherwise it will fly away."

"Mother," I said.

"Yes?"

"That old man at the next table doesn't take his eyes off of you. Who is he? Is he someone you know?"

"That's Mr. Cici," said my mother.

"Mr. Cici? Who's that? I never heard of someone like that."

"A long time ago, when I was a young girl in Iraq, Mr. Cici was a man who was in love with me."

"But he's much older than you. . . ."

"Cici was much older than me then, too," said my mother.

"Why is his name Mr. Cici?"

"My friends and I gave him that name. He gave me a "Cici" ring. All embarrassed and shy, he gave me the ring in an elegant box. We laughed a lot over it."

At once I remembered.

"The gold bow ring that had the ruby teardrop stone in the middle!"

"Yes," said my mother. "A keepsake from Cici."

I had the ring. My mother had given it to me. "When I go home I'll put it right on . . . ," I thought.

I hugged my mother, bringing her close to me. Slowly the clouds began to turn red and the day to break.

With the daylight the crowd in the Emperor Tea Garden began to fade, they began to lose their color. They began to disappear little by little.

The body and right arm of Mr. Cici, sitting at the next table, were gone now. Only his head, left hand, and left leg were visible. He lifted his cup with his left hand and took a sip of *salep,* then his left hand and head disappeared. The *salep* cup slowly settled on its saucer on the table top.

I looked at Mommy.

Her beautiful red hair was mixing with the air and slowly became invisible. Her body seemed to become transparent. I grabbed her hands.

"Mom, don't go!" I shouted. "Don't go!"

"I'm not going, I'm here," said my mother.

"But I can't see you anymore."

"You can't see me right now. I'm here. Come again tomorrow night, my child, I'll be waiting for you," she said.

The sun appeared from behind the clouds. Pink light was streaming onto the tables and chairs of the Emperor Teas Garden from the reddening clouds. I looked around. The garden was completely empty. There was no one to be seen.

"Mom!" I cried. "Mommy!"

"I'm here," said my mother's voice at my side. "Don't be afraid, I'm here. Come back tomorrow. You can tell me everything you've done. All right, go off now, go into life."

I slowly stood up from where I was sitting. My mother's chair was empty. I was as though in a dream. Every part of me was numb.

"I'll come back tomorrow!" I called out. I left the Emperor Tea Garden. I came out to the highway. I began to run with all my strength. I was running towards Ankara. I was gasping for breath, my body was covered with sweat. The intercity traffic was whizzing by me. Occasionally I passed a freight truck. So I'd found my mother in the Emperor Tea Garden, and now I had this incredible strength. When I thought of the time I had spent with her, a mad feeling of happiness coursed through my veins. I kept running faster. I felt like I was about to take off. Passing the latest model cars, I was getting close to Ankara. At breakneck speed.

I saw her from the distance.

Ankara had her arms open and was waiting for me. I arrived at the city. Out of breath, I was just about to collapse at the turn for Bilkent University when Ankara embraced me with all her strength.

She put her arms around my neck and hugged me tight because she missed me so much. I realized once more why I hadn't been able to leave this city for so many years.

On my right hand side Ulus Square, the statue, the tombs, Bent Creek, and the airport road enclosed me. On the left side Abidinpaşa, the NATO road, the hills of Öveçler, Balgat, and Çukurcuma held me tightly in. Çankaya was at the tip of my nose. I felt Tunalı Hilmi Avenue in my hair. The crowds walking down the avenue made my head itch. Kavaklıdere and Gaziosmanpaşa were flung at my neck. Gölbaşı and Oran Sitesi were on my head.

Ankara had caught me head-on. She asked, with her smoky voice, "Where've you been? You've started to go far away from me. I missed you very much, I was worried,"

"Stop, don't strangle me, I can't breathe," I said.

Ankara relaxed her arms a little.

"You keep going to Izmir and Bartin. Or don't you love me anymore? What am I missing that draws you there?" she said.

"For God's sake, leave off the jealousy!" I said.

"I can't help it, I'm jealous of you," Ankara said. "Now you've started over in Izmir and Bartin."

"Good that you reminded me," I said. "I have to go to the Taşhan. They're waiting for me there. . . ."

"Are you leaving again?" asked Ankara. Her tone was one of annoyance.

"First I'm going to get in my bed and have a good rest," I said. "Let me go so I can go home."

"If that's the way you want it," said Ankara. She opened her arms. I took a deep breath and gave a stretch. I ran home.

My African violet was in the living room, in its regular place. It had turned its leaves to the sun and shut its eyes. As it had done when we got to the hotel in Bursa together, it was taking a nap under the light beams that fell on it.

It opened its eyes and looked at me.

"How are you?" it asked.

"I'm fine. I have things to tell you. I'm exhausted," I said.

I curled up on the living room carpet and fell asleep.

$$\Longrightarrow_\bullet$$

I put on my black fur and placed my pack of cigarettes, my lighter, and the door key in my black velvet night bag. I glanced in the mirror, and freshened my lipstick. I pulled the door open and left.

The taxi was waiting for me in front of the door.

"To the Casino Venus," I said to the driver. I leaned back and started to look at the city in the darkness. A little later, I passed through the glass revolving door and entered that magical world of the Casino Venus. I took a cigarette out of my bag and put it to my lips. A silver lighter reached out and lit my cigarette.

I slowly walked through the rooms of the Casino Venus, rooms that were covered with dried-cherry colored carpeting, looking at the machines around me. I missed them. I took a plate of chips and went over to the machine with the lips, the one that I really liked. I pulled out the velvet-covered chair in front of the machine and sat down. I put the chips in the slot on the side by threes and began to push the button.

The machine was more active than I thought. It must be a day when it was giving out. It gave me a hundred points right away. I put the plate of chips to one side, and began to play with the credit that was on the machine. My eyes were on the gleaming screen in front of me.

Suddenly a pink lip appeared on the screen. The second one hadn't come. The machine wasn't going to run by itself. Just as I was about to push the button, I saw that the lip on the screen with the pink lipstick was moving slightly.

"How are you tonight?" it was asking me.

"I'm good," I said. "How are you?"

"I'm good, too," said the pink lip.

I was silent, looking at her.

"Did you recognize me?" she asked. "You probably didn't recognize me. . . ."

"Excuse me," I said. "You don't seem to be a stranger, but I couldn't figure out who you were right off."

"You've never seen me . . . ," said the pink lip. "How could you recognize me? . . . I'm Madame Kelebek, from the Emperor Tea Garden. . . ."

"Madame Kelebek!" I exclaimed in astonishment. "I recognize you. I've never seen you, but I recognize you. What are you doing here, in this machine?"

"I work here nights," said Madame Kelebek. "You know, cost-of-living . . . To continue with the nice life I've become used to."

"That's so interesting . . . ," I murmured. "I thought you were always in the Emperor Tea Garden. Are you here every night?"

"No, I don't come here every night," said Madame Kelebek. "You don't get pink lip prints on this machine every night! You know this machine, sometimes lips don't come at all."

"Yes," I said. "Sometimes I play and play and the lips never come."

"Well, those are the nights I'm in the Emperor Tea Garden," said Madame Kelebek.

"Some nights the lips come one after another," I said.

"Yes, when somebody lucky sits at the machine, I'm always here, you see. I make that person win a fortune."

"And the nights you don't come?"

"Then the person who plays loses, because no lip print comes at all," she said.

I was thinking.

"Is this a rule, Madame Kelebek? How do you know when a lucky person will sit at the machine?" I asked.

Madame Kelebek laughed.

"Coincidence, chance. . . . All these things are very simple. When I come here, the person who sits down is lucky. There's no rule. That's all there is to it," she said.

"So that's all there is . . . ," I said. "Everything is just this easy. What is called luck depends on your coming to the machine. . . ."

"Yes, that's the way it is . . . ," said Madame Kelebek. "But that's only good for this machine. The pink lip prints don't come to the other machines."

"So you determine the luck of the people who come here. With your presence or absence."

"Yes, with my lips."

The luck in the machine was Madame Kelebek, I realized.

"The nights you don't come. . . ."

"Those times I'm in the Emperor Tea Garden. There's the General there, perhaps you know. . . ." said Madame Kelebek.

"Yes, I know the General. He's writing his memoirs."

I thought of something.

"I'd like to ask you something personal."

"Please, ask."

"I was wondering, are you in the General's memoirs?"

"I wouldn't know about that," said Madame Kelebek. "The General is probably writing only his military memoirs. But if there's a part about his personal life in his memoirs, then I certainly have a place in them."

"So you don't know . . . ?"

"I don't know. The orderly would know this. He's the one actually writing the memoirs."

"Yes, the orderly knows all the memoirs."

"We should ask him . . . ," said Madame Kelebek. "I'm curious too, actually. Let's ask the General's orderly tomorrow."

"You're at the Emperor Tea Garden tomorrow, aren't you?"

"Yes, towards morning. When the Casino Venus closes I go there."

I remembered the waiter. Necati who goes over to his lover when the General and Madame Kelebek are looking at one another.

"Do you know the waiter?" I asked.

"Which waiter?"

"The waiter in the Emperor Tea Garden."

"Yes, I know him," said Madame Kelebek. "He's very hard working, he's always running around between the tables."

"You play a big role in his life, did you know that?" I asked.

Madame Kelebek was taken aback.

"I play a big role in the waiter's life? How could such a thing be?" she asked.

"You know how you and the General look at one another?"

"Yes, we look at one another. . . ."

"Well, those looks between you make an electric current. A strange extension of power. Very unusual. These are powerful looks, Madame Kelebek, you know."

"I know," she said.

"There is love, passion, sexuality, attraction in these looks."

"I know what you mean."

So the waiter goes into this current and goes over to his lover, to a bed covered with light rose colored satin pillows."

"What are you saying? A love bed!" said Madame Kelebek.

"Everything that I've said is true, Madame," I said. "The waiter goes into this different world between your glances and then comes back. And on top of that, he's become addicted to it. He wants to go there all the time."

"This is incredible!" said Madame Kelebek.

"Yes, Madame. Just as you determine whether the person sitting at this machine is lucky or not, you determine the most important moments in the life of that waiter in the Emperor Tea Garden."

So that's the way it is," said Madame Kelebek. "Luck and fate."

"Yes, it is," I said. "Luck and fate. You're able to determine both chance and fate."

"Play," she said. "Please press the button. Continue to play."

I pressed the button in front of me. The machine came alive. The gleaming screen began to move. Every time I pushed the key, lip prints kept coming. I was astonished. One after the other, time after time they came, the digital figure on the counter kept increasing, the machine turned quickly by itself many times.

My champagne had been left next to me in a long-stemmed crystal glass. I took a sip of it and pushed the key again.

I couldn't believe what I saw. Four pink lips came to the screen above the line. The machine was going to operate by itself thirty two times. Enchanting music began to play continuously. Sometimes other lips came together, increasing the number of times it would play.

I had won millions in an instant.

"You're very lucky tonight," said a girl who worked there as she passed by. "Four lips came together above the line. I've never seen that before."

The automatic operation of the machine stopped. I pushed the button and rang the bell. One of the personnel came and figured out my winnings from the counter. They brought new champagne.

The machine started to make a kind of buzzing noise.

I put the pile of money they gave me in the pocket of my evening bag.

"Thank you, Madame Kelebek," I said.

"Listen to me," said the lips with the pink lipstick. "How well do you know the General's orderly?"

"I don't know him at all. I've never even seen him. . . ."

"I know him very well," said Madame Kelebek. "He's very handsome."

"Really?"

"Yes, he's very handsome and young. He's writing his memoirs at the same time as he writes the General's."

"How can he do that?" I asked in surprise. "Don't the memories get mixed up together?"

"They do get mixed up. The General and the orderly's memories get written all mixed up in the same notebook."

"Are you sure of this?" I asked.

"I'm sure," said Madame Kelebek. "The orderly told me."

"Combined memories . . . Interesting. . . ."

"Yes. Combined memories. I don't know if I'm in the General's memoirs, but I'm in the orderly's."

"Madame . . . you didn't, with the General's orderly. . . ."

"Yes, I lived with him . . . ," said Madame Kelebek. "We would meet in a hotel room in Paris."

What I was hearing astonished me.

"Well, what about your looks at the General? That current, that love?" I asked.

"Who told you I was looking at the General?"

"But I know that electric current. I went into it myself!" I cried. "It's real."

"How did you figure out that the electric current was between me and the General?" asked Madame Kelebek.

"I saw the General's eye."

"Yes, but you didn't see the other eye."

"Which eye?"

"The orderly's eye.

"Does the orderly have an eye, too!" I shouted.

Madame Kelebek gave a sultry laugh.

"What are you saying? How could the orderly not have an eye? Of course he has one!"

"I didn't see it."

"You missed it."

"Maybe . . . ," I murmured.

"The real electric current was of course the line between me and the orderly," said Madame Kelebek.

I was totally confused.

"But when the General fell asleep the current was cut, Madame," I said. "I saw it with my own eyes. The poor waiter came back from the world he went to, flat on the ground."

"Ah," said Madame Kelebek, "You know, the looks were just acting. The waiter was caught in the vibrations between me and the orderly."

"Is that really true?" I asked.

"Yes, that's the truth," she said.

The voice coming from the machine cut off. I pushed the key once or twice. The lip prints didn't come. Madame Kelebek was gone.

I got up from my seat and went outside the Casino Venus. I was dazed from all the things I had learned. I walked slowly in the darkness.

So that sexy Madame Kelebek used to meet up with the General's orderly in a Paris hotel room once upon a time. The General had no idea. And it seemed the waiter didn't know about this affair, either.

Thinking about all this, I arrived at my house. I turned on the living room lights. My African violet looked at me as if to say, "Hi, where've you been?"

I was suddenly filled with happiness. All the irritation and humiliation had passed. It was speaking to me. It was wondering where I'd been.

I slowly sat down in the armchair next to it.

"I've been living through things that are so incredible you would never believe me if I told you, but they're real," I said. "I'll put it all together and tell you about it. I've met such unusual people, I've been in such strange worlds!"

"You'll tell me everything, won't you?" asked my violet.

"I'll tell you everything. You know, it's like I live all of this for you. To tell you. Such unusual things."

"Don't you get tired going through all this?" it asked.

"I do get tired. But I get such strong feelings. I'll tell you the whole story."

"Ok," it said. "I'm anxious to hear."

⋙∘

I was in Bartin. It must have been well past midnight. The delicate crescent moon had disappeared from the deep blue sky a while earlier.

I was in front of the Taşhan. I pushed the door open and went in.

The crowd of men inside was the same. I saw my man.

"What's up? Where were you? You haven't been here for a few nights," he said to me.

"I was busy. Away in some other places. How's it here?" I asked.

"As usual," said the man. "The illusionary women will be here soon."

I sat at a table near the back. I was looking around. Two tables ahead, a man sitting by himself caught my eye. He was good-looking, with a strange attractiveness. He must have been only about thirty. He was sitting there lost in thought, running his fingers in circles around the beer glass in front of him. He had olive skin and his black eyes seemed dreamy; staring at the door.

In a low voice, I asked the man sitting at the table behind me, "Who is this man? I've never seen him here before."

"No, you've never seen him here before. He comes once in a while. He's supposed to be some old general's orderly. He's in love with the general's lover. The woman's in love with him too. See how handsome he is. The woman will come over to him in a little while. He's waiting for her. He's very excited, you see?"

"So an old general's orderly . . . ," I said.

"Yes," said the man. "He's very noble looking, isn't he? Like a prince."

"He looks like Rudolf Valentino," I said. "The color of his skin, the lines of his face, the way his hair is combed back. . . ."

"Who did you say he looked like?" asked the man.

"An old movie actor. . . ."

"He's different from the men here, isn't he? Something other. . . ."

"Different," I said. "Really something other."

"The woman he's waiting for is different, too. You'll see in a little bit. She'll come soon. His woman's something really different," said the man. He drained his beer.

I was looking closely at the General's orderly, whom I had never seen in the Emperor Tea Garden. I was excited as I sat there: in a little while I would see Madame Kelebek, while up till now I had only seen her lips and heard her voice.

The door of the Taşhan started to open and close. The illusionary ladies gradually began to slip inside. They came silently to the tables and sat down across from the men who were waiting for them.

"There!" said the man. "She's here!"

The General's orderly sat up straight at his table. His eyes were gleaming as he looked at the door.

I turned my eyes to the door.

Madame Kelebek was standing on the threshold.

I stared for a moment at her striking, unique appearance.

Madame Kelebek had on a floor length black mink coat. Inside the coat she had on a shiny champagne colored evening gown embroidered with precious stones and pearls. Her jet black hair was gathered behind, curling over her neck in three falls that reminded one of the neck of a black swan. A very thin black tulle lace veil, like a spider's web, covered her face. I recognized her full pink lips right away. In one hand she had a worked black fan. She slowly slipped through the doorway and into the Taşhan.

"That's some woman, isn't it?" whispered my man. "She's the most extraordinary woman who's ever come into the Taşhan. In a minute she'll lift the veil covering her face and you'll be amazed how beautiful her face is. Her lips look like they were made to whisper a person's fate to them. It's so strange, it always seems like that to me."

Madame Kelebek, walking as though she were slipping through the Taşhan, went to the table of the General's orderly.

"Who is this orderly? What's his connection?" I asked the man.

Madame Kelebek sat at the table and opened her veil. A pair of deep eyes were now fixed on the eyes of the orderly.

"He's the son of a well-off family. He's been with the general for years. The General loves him like a son. They're like two halves of the same person. One of them has the attractiveness and youth, the other the maturity and wisdom. . . . They're never apart. So, they're both in love with the same woman," he said.

What the man said made me think.

"So, two halves of the same man. . . . That's so very interesting. . . . They complete one another, don't they?" One is totally handsome and young, the other is very experienced and knows everything. . . ."

"Yes," said the man. "That's what I think. They're two halves of the same man."

My eyes drifted over to the table where Madame Kelebek and the orderly were sitting. The two of them had drawn close and had started to speak in low tones to one another.

⋙●

I ran into the Casino Venus. The glass door turned behind me and closed. I looked at the machine with the lips. It was unoccupied. I got some chips and sat down in the armchair in front of the machine.

I wondered if Madame Kelebek were there. I'd know shortly. I began to push the chips in my hand into the slot three and four at a time.

There was no sign of the lips. I began to lose hope. It seemed that Madame Kelebek hadn't come to work at the Casino Venus tonight. The chips were done. I got another bowl of chips from the counter and sat down in the armchair again. I was tossing the chips three at a time into the slot.

She wasn't there. I wasn't going to find her. I lit a cigarette. I took a sip of champagne. I put three more chips in the slot.

Suddenly a pair of pink lips appeared on the moving screen of the machine.

She had come. Madame Kelebek was in front of me. Hesitantly, "Madame Kelebek?" I asked.

"Hello?" said the lips. They were out of breath.

"I was afraid you weren't going to come at all tonight. I was afraid for a minute."

"I came very quickly, but I was still late. I'm out of breath. Give me a minute," said Madame Kelebek's lips.

I put down the chips and was watching her.

"Did something happen?" I asked.

"I couldn't leave the Emperor Tea Garden," she said.

"I was concerned. Did something happen there?" I asked again.

"The waiter . . . ," she said. "You know the waiter there. . . . He just jumped into the looks between me and the orderly. He fell to the floor like he had been hit by a high voltage current. I was very frightened. His eyes were frozen. For a minute I thought he was dead. For a long time the orderly and I couldn't take our eyes off one another. So that the current would keep on coming, so that it wouldn't stop all of a sudden. Then the waiter started to blink his eyes. He sat up. It was so strange, it was as though he had the happiest smile in the world on his face. He stood and straightened himself up, then dashed off to do his work. It was only then that I could get up. I barely made it here."

"You mean the waiter went over to his lover again," I said. "He can't stand it anymore, he wants to go there every minute."

"I know," said the pink lips. "A love nest. How it draws a person. Like a huge magnet. That's why the orderly and I couldn't take our eyes away from one another. Otherwise the waiter would have stayed where he was forever. He wouldn't have been able to get back, you know what I mean? He couldn't have got that current, this vibration he dived into, from the other side."

"Right," I said. "He would have stayed there forever. Next to Hatice, on that bed with the baby pink satin pillow. . . ."

"Everything would have been ruined," said Madame Kelebek. "After a while he would have become bored there. He would have wanted to come back to the Emperor Tea Garden, to his job. Men are like that; he would have missed going around among the tables, giving out *salep*. He would have grown tired of his lover, maybe they would have had a fight. That unmatchable beauty would have turned into a dull love story. I couldn't have borne that. I didn't want to ruin that incomparable magic that the waiter was experiencing."

I was thinking.

"If the waiter stayed there, everything would become ordinary and get ruined, wouldn't it, Madame Kelebek?"

"Yes. If you don't pay attention, the thing that gets old fastest is love. Imagine that you spend your whole life lying on a bed. After a while you'd start to figure how you could get away. That love bed turns into a prison. That magic sexuality would turn its place over to loss of desire, to torture. Everything would end. Excitement and interest would die. But I didn't want the incomparable thing that the waiter had to turn into that," she said.

I was listening to her in admiration. How well she knew the world of men and women, she knew everything.

"Madame," I said. "I came here to ask you something I'm very curious about. I saw you in the Taşhan. In Bartin. . . . You were there with the orderly. You were glowing like the sun at the table, or like secret moonlight. I don't know. . . ."

"Thank you," said Madame Kelebek.

"That man is crazy in love with you. I saw that. You love him too. Well, what about the General? What place does he have in your life? I really was very curious about that."

Madame Kelebek thought for a minute.

"The General is also very important in my life," she said.

"I know that."

"The orderly is a man's springtime. High-spirited, excited, passionate . . . Like a tree that's newly in leaf. . . . The General, well, he's the fall. Yellow leaves, a thick tree attached to the earth. Quiet, steady, reliable, old. He's a harbor. Do you get what I mean?"

"I understand very well," I said. "You like to live all the seasons of a man at once."

"Yes," said Madame Kelebek. "He's the fire of love, the ring of passion, the most beautiful sexual attraction. But sometimes antagonizing. Because these are very strong feelings. Jealous, demanding, impatient. But the General is like a still lake . . . Understanding and forgiving."

"Or is it that you're afraid of love, Madame Kelebek," I asked. "You're dividing your love in two. You're afraid, aren't you?"

The machine's shiny screen suddenly started to turn. The pink lips were lost now. Madame Kelebek hadn't wanted to answer my question.

"She ran away . . . ," I whispered. I lit a cigarette. I got up from in front of the machine, and passing through the glass doors, left the Casino Venus.

≫•

"Where've you been?" cried Gül Abla. "Where are you these days? I haven't seen you for two days. If you knew what's been going on in your absence. . . ."

I sat down across from Gül Abla in the velvet armchair with the wooden arms.

"What happened, Gül Abla?" I asked.

"One of my African violets dried up," she said. Her voice was pained.

My eyes went to the violets on the table.

"Which one? Which one dried up?" I asked with concern.

"That one sitting in front of the window, my oldest violet. It didn't bloom. Just sat there angrily staring outside. It suddenly dried up. I couldn't save it."

"I ran my eyes over the African violets on the table. Gül Abla got up from her seat and went to the kitchen. I heard her sobbing.

"Gül Abla!"

"Wait, I'm coming," she said.

The violet with the broad leaves was in its place.

"Şakir Bey, what happened?" I asked.

"Don't ask," said Şakir Bey. "Rıza went, just like that. May God give you life. He'd had a lot to drink again, depressed. In the morning we looked, and he was dead. We lost him. Who knows, maybe it was the best thing for him," he said.

"And Gül Abla? What did she do?"

"She fell apart. It's so strange, she's been crying all day. And I thought she didn't love Rıza Bey. So, you had some strange connection with him. Well, he was her husband all those years. She sat at the table and cried and cried."

"Where's the pot now?" I asked.

"They took it to the garden after the noon prayer," said Şakir Bey.

Gül Abla came into the room. Her eyes, swollen from crying, were all red.

"He went before I could talk to him, before I could explain things to him, Rıza," she said. "I'll never see him again. It's so painful!. . . . I didn't tell him things that I should have told him for years. We never spoke enough to one another. I think, now, how he's gone and left in that atmosphere of all the things we didn't say to one another. Words, a simple sentence, a remark that leaves an imprint . . . none of them exist anymore. They were never used. But I was going to say some things to him. I feel so guilty!"

Gül Abla began to sob again.

"Listen to me," she said. "When a person is still alive, you should say everything to them that you want to say. Later it's too late. I feel so helpless."

The old telephone on the low table rang. Gül Abla reached out and picked up the phone.

"It's for you. A man."

I took the receiver in my hand.

"Hello," I said.

"Hello, this is Irfan, the Paradise guard," said the voice on the other end. "Are you there?"

"Yes, I'm with Gül Abla. She lost her husband."

"I know," said Irfan. "Rıza Bey is next to me. I'm taking him to the Emperor Tea Garden."

"To the Emperor Tea Garden?"

"Yes. He's getting used to the new situation little by little."

"How is Rıza Bey?" I asked with interest.

"He's just fine. He's not drinking. He's come to himself."

"So he's not drinking."

"He's not drinking. He told me a little while ago that he sees the world differently now."

"Is he going right now to the Emperor Tea Garden?"

"Yes. If Gül Hanım wants to, she can see him there."

The line was cut. I put down the phone.

Gül Abla was looking at me with concern.

"Who was that you spoke to? I heard you say Rıza," she said.

"Come," I said to Gül Abla.

"Where?" she asked.

"Put something on and come, Gül Abla. We're going towards Izmir."

"Towards Izmir."

"Yes. We're going to the Uşak intersection, to the Emperor Tea Garden."

≈₀

What I had seen had seen had shaken me, completely astonished me. I stayed where I was for a minute. The Casino Venus game machines with their multicolored lights seemed to be whirring away all around me. My stomach was turning. A cold sweat filled my whole body. But it was as cool as always inside the Casino Venus.

The machine with the lips was in front of me. A woman was sitting in the armchair where I always sat. A pair of pink lips appeared on the screen. I instantly recognized them as Madame Kelebek's lips.

The woman leaned forward and was talking to the lips in a low voice. She must have asked something, and now the pink lips were answering her.

Madame Kelebek was talking to someone else just as she had spoken to me.

I got closer to them. I was trying to hear what they were saying.

Madame Kelebek's lips were saying, "Yes, Paris that season seemed enchanted. I felt like I was in a dream. I spent the all that day wandering through the streets feeling as though I had drunk champagne, and passed my nights in his arms in that little hotel room, listening to the fiery words he was whispering in my ear."

The woman asked, "Were you very young when you met the General, Madame?"

"I was just a child," Madame Kelebek answered her. "In a music hall revue I would get on a white pony and ride around the stage. I tossed out red roses from a basket I had in my hand. The General saw me one night and caught one of the roses that I threw. . . ."

≫⊙

The woman noticed me. She suddenly turned. We came eye to eye.

She must have seen in my eyes that jealousy I couldn't hide, that I was struggling with at that moment.

I recognized her eyes, too. My eyes remained fixed at the pair of icy blue eyes that were staring at me.

Sabriye.

Sabriye's eyes that I hadn't seen for years, hadn't thought about, had long since forgotten, eyes that were buried somewhere in my childhood. . . .

These eyes were the eyes of the former lover of a man I had fallen in love with when I was still young enough to be called a child. At that moment my whole life passed in front of me: My mother, my father, the mansion we lived in in Kızıltoprak, the Kalamış Dock, the burning pain of first love like a smooth dagger planted in the heart, memories that had long since been carried away by the years, the city I left behind, all suddenly piled on top of me.

A moment when I flew back to the days when I didn't understand people very well, to times when it didn't even occur to me to see my rights, to Istanbul which I fled, leaving everything behind like a worn-out wind. . . .

It was as though I lived again that strange day when I first saw this pair of blue eyes, the day that I ran into the person I loved with the conviction and purity of a child, when he was with his other lover, the park decorated with flower beds next to the Moda Beach, Koco's Taverna a little down below, with its glass booths for sitting.

Seconds passed like years. Those icy blue eyes stared straight at me. I couldn't decide for a moment whether I was in the Casino Venus or in that park in Moda Bay from years ago. It was like that stretch we call life was caught between our looks, and time and place had been erased.

Was I still a child; had I not experienced any of the things I later lived through? I was full of such strange feelings. As though those blue eyes had nailed me to a sunny early evening in the past. I could neither go forward nor backward. I was stuck in the slice of past time.

Sabriye's eyes. . . .

They had ruined all my childhood dreams, beliefs, and love that beautiful sunny evening in Moda Park years and years ago, in the hours when everyone was happy, among the park benches and the yellow flowers where the bees alighted. . . .

"I love him too, he's mine. He loves me too," she had said to me.

And yes, the same blue eyes were looking at me with hatred again.

There, I felt like that child whose world had been destroyed years ago, and I slowly pulled myself together.

We weren't in Moda Park, we were in the Casino Venus.

"Were you playing the machine?" I asked.

With a cold voice, "I was talking to Madame Kelebek," she said.

We recognized one another, but we pretended that we didn't. I understood this terrible game.

When we first met, too, she was as closed and withdrawn as I was open. Years ago, I was put in the position of the guilty party in Moda Park. I couldn't fight, I couldn't defend myself. But my world was the real one.

An old lover was accusing me, but I didn't know life, and my world was destroyed. The real guilty part was the man between us, and I understood his weakness. I hated both of them for a time, and I fled from that city, leaving my youth behind.

How strange, here she was again.

Sabriye. . . .

"Do you know Madame Kelebek?" I asked.

"Yes, I know her. She's my friend," she replied. She opened up her purse, took out a cigarette and lit it.

We were following one another. She had crow's feet around her eyes, and had aged a little.

"Madame Kelebek is a very unusual woman," I said. Just to say something.

"Yes, Madame Kelebek, the orderly, the General . . . they're all very unusual," said Sabriye.

"You know them. . . ."

"I know them," she said. "I'm researching their lives."

"Why? Why are you researching these people's lives?" I asked.

She blew a puff of cigarette smoke away.

"I'm writing a novel," she said.

I was terrified for a minute.

"You're writing a novel?" I was able to say. It was hard for me to speak.

"Yes, I'm writing a novel."

"Who are the other characters? Are they all unusual, out-of-the-ordinary people?"

"There are African violets," she said. "Illusionary women . . . a placed called the Taşhan in Bartin . . . An old woman named Gül Hanım . . ."

"Celal . . . ," I whispered. "Is he in it, too?"

"Of course he is," she said. "Adviye, Mebrure, Gül Hanım's African violet men . . . The Paradise guard Irfan . . . The Emperor Tea Garden . . . The waiter there. . . ."

Suddenly I lost control of myself.

I screamed with all my might.

"Thief! Thief! Leave my world alone! You can't take my world from me, you thief! They're all mine. You can't understand them, you thief!"

My voice echoed in the Casino Venus, on the velvet covered places, the lit up ceilings, and the colored screens on the machines.

"You're the thief!" she said. "You're the real thief. Did you forget years ago? You took from me the man who made my world and my existence. You're the thief!"

"Thief! Thief!"

I didn't even know whose throat this scream came from.

When I opened my eyes, I realized that I had been laid on a long lounge chair covered with black velvet. They had covered me with my fur. Still I was trembling like someone with malaria.

Someone gave me a glass of water. I slowly sat up and drank the water. Madam Kelebek was at my side. She was looking at me with concern in her eyes.

"What happened? Where am I?" I asked.

"You had a nightmare. An attack. It passed. It's all over now," said Madame Kelebek. Drink a little more water."

"A nightmare? I wasn't sleeping! How could I have a nightmare?"

"You weren't sleeping, but you were fooling around with dreams," said Madame Kelebek. "Things like this happen. It's over. It's not important. Your subconscious played a bad trick on you."

"Where's the woman with the blue eyes who was speaking to you, Madame Kelebek?" I asked.

"What woman with blue eyes?"

"She was talking to you. You were telling her about Paris."

"When?"

"When I came into the Casino Venus."

"I wasn't talking to anyone," said Madame Kelebek.

"But I saw her. She was real. Sabriye. She came into my world. She said everything one by one. She's writing a novel, she said."

"I told you it was a nightmare," said Madame Kelebek. "Don't think about it. Rest a little. There's no such person."

"There is, there's such a person," I insisted.

Madame Kelebek leaned over and looked in my eyes.

"There is no such person. You just thought there was. You had a fright. You thought your world was disappearing from between your fingers. Sleep a little, rest. You're exhausted," she said.

"There isn't such a person. . . ."

"No."

I leaned my head back and closed my eyes. Then I realized how tired I was. I was worn out.

"There's no such person, right?" I whispered.

"No. How could there be?" said Madame Kelebek.

"Okay," I said slowly. I drifted off.

I felt that Madame Kelebek was softly patting my hands. Her hands were so soft.

Suddenly I opened my eyes.

⇛o

"What happened?" Gül Abla asked. "I'm ready. You were going to take me someplace."

I looked around. I was in Gül Abla's little room with the window seat.

"Was I here all the time, Gül Abla?" I asked.

"Where would you be? You were here. You passed out in the chair. You're wearing yourself out these days. Relax a little. You won't be able to keep on like this," said Gül Abla.

I was suspicious. What I had just experienced was real. I didn't believe what Madame Kelebek and Gül Abla said. Had Madame Kelebek really just been by my side? Everything was all mixed up in my head.

They had both been there and they were both real. I was meeting them in different dimensions; I was living in different worlds.

Sabriye. . . .

Those icy blue eyes suddenly came to my mind.

She was real too, I knew.

I was full of suspicion. She was about to take over my world, my people. Maybe she already had. How had I not realized before this. . . .

"What are you thinking?" said Gül Abla.

"Sabriye."

"Who's that?"

"Don't you know her?"

"No, I've never heard of anyone like that. . . ."

"But she talked about you. . . ."

"I don't know anyone like that. Who is she?" asked Gül Abla.

"Somebody from the past, from long ago. I'd forgotten all about her. A woman. She was a girl once . . . Sabriye . . . ," I said. "She suddenly showed up. It was as though she had all the keys to my life in her hand, she was talking to my people, she knew them. She knew places that were just mine, but, oddly enough, these were people and places that had been created by loneliness. There's no way for her to know and analyze them all.

I can't believe it, how could something like this happen, how could Sabriye get into this dimension? I left her way behind in the past and fled long ago," I said.

Gül Abla was listening carefully to me.

"You never told me about this Sabriye," she said.

"She wasn't someone in my life! I hadn't thought of her for maybe twenty years. What could I say about her?" I said.

"But you didn't forget her," said Gül Abla. "She was in your subconscious, obviously. She suddenly came out. Forget about it, don't think about her."

"What if she takes over my world?"

"No, dear, she can't take over your world. Come on, let's go."

We turned off the light and went outside.

The Emperor Tea Garden was empty, as always. Gül Abla and I went in the gate.

"It's morning," said Gül Abla. "Let's sit down at a table and relax. The trip tired me."

We sat at one of the tables.

The waiter appeared.

"Welcome. What would you like?" he asked.

"I'd like a nice tea," said Gül Abla. "It's so quiet here."

"I'll have a tea too," I said to the waiter.

Gül Abla was carefully looking around.

"Look," she said. "Someone left her evening bag on that empty table over there."

I instantly recognized Madame Kelebek's purse. She must be sitting at the table.

"Let me go wash my hands before the waiter brings the tea," I said. I went to the kitchen in the back of the tea garden. The smell of freshly brewed tea filled the little shack. The waiter was next to the propane tank. He was getting the glasses ready.

Suddenly I saw her.

Sabriye.

She was sitting in a corner of the kitchen. Her icy blue eyes were fixed on me. I recoiled.

"Sabriye!" I said.

"You recognized me, didn't you?" she said.

"As soon as I saw you I knew you. In the Casino Venus. When you were sitting at the machine with the lips."

"Come here, I want to talk to you. That's why I came here," she said.

I pulled up a chair and sat next to her.

"How do you know where I am, and the people that I know, Sabriye?" I asked. "Weren't you and I people from very different worlds? When our lives collided with each other that day in Moda Park we never really even spoke to one another. . . ."

"We didn't know about life . . . ," said Sabriye. Her blue eyes softened. "I was never happy with him, you know?" she said. "I left my house, I ran away. I left him."

"But you loved him so much," I said. "'I can't live without you!' you said to him. You told me. After I left town you got married. . . ."

"I had very unhappy years," said Sabriye. "Don't be hard on me. I paid a lot for that mistake. You were actually the lucky one. You picked up and left. . . ."

"I left my world behind when I went . . . ," I said. "My family, the Istanbul that I was crazy about, the Kalamış pier, the tea you drink in the 'luxury class' on the ferryboats, my books, my furniture, Nişantaşı and Harbiye where I spent my childhood, the boats to the islands, Lifter's Taverna in Beyoğlu, which I absolutely loved, the attic flat in Kızıltoprak, everything I loved, I left everything I had behind when I took a midnight train and left town never to come back."

"I know," she said.

"That gentle climate, the wisteria blooming in the spring, fried mussels you eat on the Bosphorus, the *kokoreç,* the theater lobbies I loved, the university, the old tree in the courtyard that I loved so much, I left them all to you. The trams, the creek with the frogs, the flowers bending out over the balconies, that incredible view from Seraglio Point, old Istanbul . . . Everything. . . . Did you use them, Sabriye? Did you put yourself in my world?"

"Who knows . . . ," she said. "It was years ago." She was pensive.

"Nobody can erase themselves from a world like that. But I did it," I said.

She was silent.

"What are you looking for now in this world that belongs to me? How did you find me years later? We are two people with completely separate roads. This world. This tea garden, the people in it, the machine with the pink lips, they're mine. Leave them alone!" I said. "I left you everything. Don't touch them, don't bother them. I never came after you on the road you took. I left you all the rowboats at the Kalamış Pier, the sunsets, the mimosas in the gardens of the old wooden mansions, the open-air cinemas, my first youth, my dreams. . . . What are looking for here?"

Sabriye's blue eyes teared over.

"You're heartless," she said. "You never forgave me. I realize that. But my life wasn't happy and pleasant the way you think. I came to tell you that."

"I don't care about your life!" I said. "You picked out your own life. Why are you telling me all of this after all these years?"

"I don't know," said Sabriye. "I just am. . . . I felt I had to tell you all this sometime in my life, some night." She wrinkled up her face. "That was an awful night." She murmured. "I left everything behind, too. How strange: I thought of you. That kid standing in front of me in Moda Park. That kid trying to talk to me, who I listened to in silence. . . . I thought of you."

"Strange," I said. "If I hadn't heard it straight from you I would never have believed it. How do you know about this garden?"

She looked into my eyes.

"I've been here in this garden for a while," she said. "In the mornings I sit at a table right here and get some sun. I look at the traffic going by on the highway for a while and have a tea."

I stared at her.

Sabriye went on.

"I know all of these people, your people, from this garden. I followed behind you and I learned every place you went. I found the Casino Venus. I got to know the machines there, I walked around the Taşhan."

"You mean you followed me like a shadow?"

"Yes," she said. "Like a shadow. . . ."

"All right: why?"

"I was curious. I've been curious for years. I wanted to know what kind of person you were."

She slowly seemed to be turning transparent. First her body became like a cloud, then the yellow dress she had on faded and disappeared.

"Sabriye!" I shouted.

Her blue eyes were still there. She was looking at me.

"I'm here," she said.

"Sabriye, you aren't. . . ."

"Yes," she said softly.

"When?"

"A few years ago. . . ."

"How strange, I didn't hear. . . ."

"How would you hear. . . . I thought of you that night. As I was leaving everything. . . ."

A feeling of sadness came over me.

Sabriye was no longer there. The smell of the fresh tea the waiter had brewed filled the little shack.

Suddenly a strange thing happened. Night . . . Night came!

He was in a good mood. Trailing behind him were the sounds of night guards' whistles, drunken songs, the laughter of sexy ladies, the howling of dogs and the wind hitting the branches of the trees. . . .

"Here I am!" he said. He was full of fun.

Everything suddenly went dark.

The waiter shouted in amazement. "It just turned into night. But it was morning just a minute ago. What weird things are going on!" He turned off the gas.

Night whispered in my ear, "Come on, let's go out and have some fun. We'll take a walk. You're all down, bored. I can tell by looking at you. Let's go someplace fun," he said.

"Let's go, but I have so many things to do!" I said.

"Like what?" he asked.

"There are so many people I have to see, to talk to. They're waiting to hear from me. People I have to take places, people I have to connect with one another. . . ."

"Why is it up to you? Let them find what they need for themselves!" said Night.

I thought for a moment.

"Right!" I said.

"You know your guy?" said Night.

"Yeah, what?"

"He loves you."

"How do you know?" I asked in excitement.

"He loves you a lot. Last night I was in your house. We talked," he said. "He keeps to himself. He doesn't talk about himself much, you know."

"I know," I said.

"He's a different kind of lover, your guy," said Night. "He told me great things. He worries about you when you go to the Casino Venus."

"He came to the Casino Venus three or four times," I said.

"He came to see you. He told me. He saw the machines. The machines you play. . . ."

"Let's go to him," I said impatiently.

"He's asleep now. Let him sleep," said Night.

"Where should we go?" I asked.

"Wherever you want," said Night. I felt an indescribable feeling of joy and freedom inside.

"I want to go back to the Emperor Tea Garden. The people there. . . ."

"Of course you'll go back there. Those people are always there. Nothing ever stops existing. You know this by now," he said.

"I know," I said. "I know now that nothing ceases to exist."

"Come on," said Night. "I'll introduce you to someone."

"Leave off, for God's sake. The last thing I want to do is to meet someone new right now. I've met so many people recently. I'm worn out," I said.

Night said, "But this is someone different, very different."

"They're all different aren't they?"

"Yes, but this one I'm going to introduce you to is really unique. You have to meet him."

"Who is it?"

"You'll see, right now!"

Night was moving swiftly along the roads. I was following behind. We turned into Arjantin Avenue. We stopped in front of a little secluded bar. I looked at the name. It said NIGHT BAR.

"Let's go in. He's waiting."

"Okay."

We went inside the bar.

A young man was sitting at one of the side tables. When he saw us come in he straightened up a little in his seat.

I was mesmerized for a minute. Something like an electric shock went through my body. He was handsome, with an attitude I wasn't familiar with. I could see he was very attractive. He smiled a little at me. His dark eyes were gleaming; he was young, but he was staring at me like someone who had seen a lot, done a lot. He was excited too. I caught that.

Night said," Let me introduce you." Indicating the young man to me, he added, "You already know him, anyway."

"We probably haven't met."

"Well, then I'll introduce you. Your novel."

I was astonished.

"Who?" I managed to say.

"Your novel," said Night. "Didn't you recognize him? That's your novel."

The young man stuck out his hand, smiling.

"My name is The Emperor Tea Garden," he said. "I'm your novel that you're about to finish. I wanted to meet you very much. You've been working on me for four months. Maybe I tired you out, but I didn't want to. But you created me. I'm ready to meet the reader with all the action, people, and different times and places that I have inside me. I'm very excited."

"So you're my novel, *The Emperor Tea Garden*," I murmured.

I was stunned.

"Yes," he said.

We sat down at the table.

My novel was sitting across from me. I looked straight at him. "You're so independent; when I was writing you, you dragged me from here to there, didn't obey any of the rules, and paid no attention to what I said, you know. You dragged me from place to place and left me there. Sometimes I couldn't control you. The characters in you sometimes jumped out like they were spilling from a package, they astonished me."

"I know," he said. "We've lived together the last four months. I know all of your feelings, your thoughts, and your conflicts. You made me up out of them."

"What are we drinking?" said Night.

"Let's have whiskey," I said. I lit a cigarette.

"I'm sorry that I'm being finished," said my novel. "In a little while you'll finish me. You'll put the last period down. When I felt this I got upset."

"What do you mean you felt it?"

"How would I not feel it, I realized right away," he said. "I don't want to leave you."

"You'll belong to others."

"Yes, but I don't want to leave you. I've learned your world. When you put the last dot down and put down your pen I don't know what I'll do."

"What a strange situation," I murmured. "I never knew novels had feelings of their own."

"You're full of feelings. You transferred your feelings to me," said the novel.

I was drinking my whiskey. I was deep in thought.

"Do you remember, you started to write my first pages in a tea garden in Gölbaşı," he said. "Autumn had begun. The lake was still. There were ducks around. . . ."

"I remember," I said.

"Now we've come to the end of everything. Now I'll leave you. It's painful," he said.

His eyes were on mine.

"Everything is inside of you," I said. "All of the people I love, the events, the places. All of it. . . ."

"I know. The Emperor Tea Garden, the Taşhan, Madame Kelebek, the General, the waiter, Sabriye, your mother . . . Gül

Hanım. The latest Japanese gambling machines that you're so fond of. . . ."

"You're ready to live, aren't you?" I asked him.

"I'm ready," he said. He polished off his whiskey.

"Well, I bid you farewell," I said. "Have a good journey. I wish you good luck."

My novel got to his feet. He took my two hands firmly.

"Be well," he said. "I'm going now. With all the characters inside me. I'm leaving like a ship leaving port with its load."

He got to the door of the bar in two minutes. He stopped there, turned, and looked at me for the last time. Then he went out the door. He was lost in the darkness.

"The novel is finished," said Night.

I was distracted.

"Yes, the novel is finished."

"He'll go on his own road now. . . ."

"Yes."

"Are you unhappy?"

"I'm sad. I've been separated from my people. I won't be able to see them anymore, I won't be able to go to those places anymore."

"He's unhappy too. He's unhappy to part from you."

"It's not easy, we did everything together for the last few months."

Night called the waiter. He paid the bill. We got up from the table and left the bar.

Inside me there was an emptiness, a diminishing.

"I think I'll go home and lie down a bit," I said to Night. "The novel is finished. There's nothing left to write now."

"You can go to the movies and things in the daytime," said Night.

"That's probably what I'll do."

"Are you going to gamble tonight?"

"I don't know. Maybe I will play a little."

Night stared at me.

"You've fallen for him, haven't you?" he asked.

I was silent for a moment.

"I don't know, maybe," I said.

"I realized from the way you looked," said Night. "A strange love. . . ."

"See you tomorrow," I said. I ended it.

I got home. I opened the door with my key and lit the lights in the living room.

My African violet was looking at me.

"It's over," I said. The novel just ended a little while ago."

"I know," it said. "You're tired, but it turned out well."

I went into my bedroom.

The red light on my answering machine was flashing.

I pressed the button. The voice of my novel came from the little tape cassette and filled my room.

"Be well. I love you," it said.

For a minute I thought hopelessly how I would get to him, where I could find him. He hadn't left a number; I didn't know where he was. The doors to that world were closed now; my novel had gone off into the night.

I pressed the button and listened to the sound on the tape again.

"Be well. I love you."

1 February 1997
Ankara

GLOSSARY

Abla: Older sister, a familiar form of address to a friend

Anıtkabir: Ataturk's tomb in Ankara

Arzum: My Desire, a hotel

Asansör: Elevator—an outdoor elevator in downtown Izmir

Asmalı: Vine, a street name

Bey: Mister, sir, polite form of address

Canlı Balık: Live Fish, a restaurant

Cici: Cute, a nickname

çardak: A lean-to in a field or along a road

Çınar: Plane Tree, a restaurant

çupra: Lumpfish

Dario Moreno: Famous romantic singer of Izmir

Evliya Çelebi: Famous seventeenth-century Ottoman traveler and writer

Hanım: Lady, polite form of address

han: A caravansaray or warehouse

Hayat: Life, a hotel

ispirito: Grain alcohol

Kandil: (Candle) A Moslem religious holiday when mosques are illuminated

Kandil simidi: Holiday pastry, rather like an unsalted pretzel

Kandil simitler: Plural form of *Kandil simidi*

Kelebek: Butterfly, a character's name

kilim: A flatweave carpet

kokoreç: Roasted sweetbreads, snack food sold on the street

"Makber": "Tomb"—a well-known romantic song

rakı: Anisette-flavored Turkish national alcoholic drink, like ouzo

salep: Fermented millet, a hot winter drink, like cocoa

Sülüs: A writing style of Ottoman calligraphy distinguished by long elegant tails on letters

Taşhan: A stone caravansaray, a place name

NAZLI ERAY was born in Ankara, Turkey. After attending the English Girls Secondary School, İstanbul Arnavutköy American Girls College, and İstanbul University Faculty of Law, she started to work as a translator in the Turkish Ministry of Tourism and Promotion.

When her twin daughters were born, she left her life as a civil servant and directed herself towards literature, which she had been interested in ever since childhood. She had entered the world of literature with her story entitled "Monsieur Hristo," which she wrote when she was just a secondary school student. Her stories started to be published in the review named *Entity* one year later, and in important literary reviews such as *Turkish Language, Constitution, Yazko Literature, Demonstration,* and *Essay* after 1973. In 1975, her first book, entitled *Ay Bayim Ah,* was published.

In 1986, an anthology consisting of her stories was published in Germany. Her stories, plays and novels have been translated into English, French, German, Italian, Japanese, Czech, Urdu, Hindi, Swedish, and Arabic. Her novel *Orpheus* was published in the USA in English translation in 2006. Her novels *The Street of Different Dreams* and *Orpheus* are being translated into Korean.

Nazlı Eray is the founder of the (Turkish) Literary Association, a member of the Turkish Writers' Union, an honorary faculty member at Iowa University, and a member of PEN International. She has been a columnist in the Turkish newspapers *Güneş, Cumhuriyet, Radikal,* and *Akşam.* Eray speaks English and French.

AMBASSADOR ROBERT FINN is the author of the book *The Early Turkish Novel,* which has been published both in English and Turkish. His poems and translations have appeared in the United States, Turkey, France, and Pakistan. The University of Texas Press published his translation of Nazlı Eray's novel *Orpheus* in 2006. He has also translated Orhan Pamuk's *The Silent House* (Knopf, 2012). He co-edited *Building State and Security in Afghanistan* (LISD-WWS-2007 and LISD 2010) with Wolfgang Danspeckgruber. Ambassador Finn holds a B.A. in American Literature and European History from St. John's University, New York, an M.A. in Near Eastern Studies from New York University, and an M.A. and Ph.D. in Near Eastern Studies from Princeton University. He was a Peace Corps volunteer in Turkey and a Fulbright scholar at Istanbul University.

Ambassador Finn is currently a visiting scholar at Columbia University. Prior to that, he was Senior Research Scholar in the Liechtenstein Institute at the Woodrow Wilson School of International Affairs of Princeton University, and Lecturer in the Woodrow Wilson School. From 2005-2008 he was also a lecturer in the Department of Near Eastern Studies at Princeton University, and he was the Ertegun Visiting Professor of Turcology at Princeton University from 2001–2002 and 2003–2005. He served as the first U.S. Ambassador to Afghanistan in more than 20 years, from March 2002 until August 2003, and as U.S. Ambassador to Tajikistan, 1998–2001. His other diplomatic postings include Istanbul, Ankara, and Izmir, Turkey; Lahore, Pakistan; and Zagreb, Croatia. He opened the U.S. Embassy in Azerbaijan in 1992. He has received numerous awards from the Government of the United States, including two Presidential Meritorious Service Awards and the US Department of State award for heroism.